@yellowcrocs421

Cancel Culture Has a Body Count, And It's Just Getting Started

Kevin Forrest Igo

IgoArt
~ LLC ~

- 2 -

This page intentionally left blank

Disclaimer

This is a work of fiction. All characters, names, organizations, brands, and events are either the product of the author's imagination or are used in a fictitious manner for storytelling purposes. Any resemblance to actual persons, living or dead, or actual events is purely coincidental.

Trademark Acknowledgment: The word "Crocs" as referenced in the title @YellowCrocs421 and use of vector image are registered trademarks of Crocs, Inc. Any mention of the brand in this work is used solely for fictional and illustrative purposes. No sponsorship, endorsement, or affiliation with Crocs, Inc. is intended or implied.

All other trademarks, product names, company names, or logos cited herein are the property of their respective owners. The inclusion of such names is not intended to infringe upon any trademark or intellectual property rights. Their use is strictly in a literary and descriptive context as part of a fictional narrative.

Acknowledgements

I wholeheartedly acknowledge my wife of 40 years, Charlotte, who has encouraged me to write for years. She is tireless. She is determined. And she is, first and foremost, my greatest champion.

As I neared the end of the writing process, I enrolled in the valued assistance of a cover designer and an editor. Paul Blane not only edited the manuscript multiple times, but being a higher education instructor I learned so much from his detailed guidance.

Nusrat Abbas Awan (Nusrat Designer) did some fantastic work with the covers, a skill set that I simply do not possess.

My adult children offered a lot of encouragement but have yet to read the book. I'm not sure I want them to, as you will soon learn why. @yellowcrocs421 is a bit of a cautionary tale that readers of thriller/crime fiction will really appreciate. I'm not sure I'm ready to answer the question: *"Is this really a story about you? Could you do this?"*

For everyone involved, I say thank you. Thank you for your patience and understanding of the mental roadblocks that I got in the way of writing. Thank you for the insights that made their way into the book. And thank you, Charlotte, for being there for all these many decades.

Dedication

This work of fiction (and it is fiction, so don't arrest me) was produced with constant affirmation and encouragement from my wife and best friend, Charlotte. We've been together since 1985 and not a day goes by that she doesn't brighten my otherwise gloomy outlook on life with her infectiously positive and sunny disposition. Without her, I would indeed be like the main character you will meet below. She centers me and literally keeps me out of trouble. During the development of this book, I also went through some rough moments with alcohol. She stayed by my side as I went through my transition to sobriety. Sadly, writing this probably took two years longer than it should have because of my habit. For her unwavering support and everlasting love, this book is dedicated to her.

About the Author

Kevin Forrest Igo is one of the most up-and-coming authors of this age. He…no, wait. I'll forego the usual sycophantic, third-person drivel one might expect to read here. I'm an average husband and father. I like scotch and the Internet, and sometimes I consume too much of both.

I'm old enough to have watched social media go from message boards on AOL dial-up to an enormous variety of apps on a smartphone. My phone is about a bazillion times more powerful than my original Intel 386, and the Internet is available at speeds that once seemed impossible. People, though, are more or less the same.

The human brain and the social fabric that we all share haven't really changed all that much. As a result, we've invented a vast host of fresh problems. In this book, I focus on how the mob has moved from the streets with pitchforks to the ease of the Web. I hope that you, dear reader, will take this cautionary tale to heart. I know I have.

PROLOGUE

"Meet KatMeow! She's the daughter of this fascist! She was there and didn't lift a finger. A baby fascist! Bonus points to anyone who can find her."

Amber Hardy (@AHardOne)

Amber and her friends left the Diamondback's baseball game as the last out was called. It had been a normal outing for the trio, with Jennifer getting completely wasted on $14 margaritas and then pulling up her shirt to expose her voluptuous breasts to the game crowd camera. Misty played her role as the slightly stoned paranoid that she was and made the group move to empty seats to avoid being located by the cops as if moving seats would help. But, since this type of mayhem was routine in a game, the cops really didn't care. Regardless, the gang had posted most of their debauchery across several platforms, so finding them would be easy for the cops, again, if they cared.

Amber was probably the more mature girl of the group, and 'The Girls,' as they called themselves, relied upon her to keep them out of trouble. Sometimes, it worked out. Sometimes, it didn't. Tonight, with a drunk Jennifer in tow, they navigated through the thousands of fans, snaking their way through the blusterous throng of drunks and obnoxious sea of bros.

"Okay, girls, I will text you all later about our plans tomorrow. Sorry again about coming late. I just couldn't get out of work," Amber said, still holding Jennifer upright and moving forward.

As they made it through the outer stadium doors, Jennifer put her arms around her friends. "Hey, why do you guys have stripper names? Did your dads have a favorite one they visited? What did your moms think?"

Amber and Misty looked at each other and smiled. They knew that when Jennifer was this toasted, there was no point in really talking to her. She'd never remember anything anyhow. Since the beginning of the game, Jennifer had become more and more nonsensical with each drink.

"Okay, Jennifer, it's time to go home now," Amber said. "I think you can walk the rest of the way with Misty, don't you?"

"Misty, the stripper?" Jennifer slurred and flapped her arms like a drunken fool.

Misty rolled her eyes and took Jennifer's hand. "Yes, Misty, the stripper is taking you to the car."

"I can drive! I'm okay. Really. I'll drive!" Jennifer shouted, attracting a crowd. It was never a good idea for a drunk girl to be in a sports crowd alone, so the girls kept Jen in tow.

"Come on, Jen, I'm driving. It's my car, you can ride shotgun! How's that?" Misty suggested as she nodded at Amber for her not to worry.

Amber let go of Jennifer's sweaty hand and had to pull it away with some force. "Hey, I'm sorry I couldn't ride with y'all. Like I said, my job got in the way. I'll find my way to my car, you two, be safe!"

Jen and Misty staggered off toward Misty's car in the nearby parking garage. Amber had to park on a surface street several blocks away since she arrived after the game had begun and well into the third inning. Her barista job was great, but sometimes, getting out on time was a chore. This time the delay was because she had to clean up the bathroom where some homeless person, or as Amber phrased it, *'a person experiencing homelessness'*, had left feces and needles all over the floor. For Amber, it was a truly horrible experience, but she did it because she really loved her shop and loved keeping it clean for her customers. The Roasted Beanie's logo featured a coffee bean with a beanie on top, and the café was a neighborhood go-to for coffee. And she was part of that success.

Amber walked down the long series of stairs to street level. There were people everywhere she looked since there was only one real exit from the stadium. She stood on the rounded corner to get her bearings and saw a long line of pedicabs waiting for passengers.

She pondered getting a pedicab, one of those three-wheeled people movers, usually helmed by a scruffy, drug-addled peddler. Some were nice, yes, but many looked, well…*rough.* However, the thought of walking on dark streets for blocks and blocks encouraged her decision to run the gauntlet and join the line.

In the pedicab line, she noticed a man holding up a large sign with her name on it. As she walked over, the man lowered the sign and waved to her.

"Amber? Your friend Misty told me you parked a long way away because you were late. She paid for a ride back to your car. She has my personal cell, as I've given her rides before. I wasn't supposed to tell you who, so don't out me until she brings it up," the man snickered a bit and directed Amber into the plastic-lined cart.

Amber looked at the man and thought he seemed safe enough. He didn't have any hair—Like at all. That was weird, but it was always hot in Arizona, being a desert and all, so people did shave a lot, especially if they worked outside. A head bandanna seemed to be mandatory for the pedicab riders, and the man had a red one, Crips style.

"Why the plastic on the seats?" Amber asked, looking just a bit nervous.

"It's easy to clean. This has fabric seats and they're impossible to sanitize. I use this here watered-down bleach between rides. Keeps your butt safer, I think," he said, sloshing the bleach jug.

That actually put Amber more at ease, and as she sat down, she picked up a whiff of the bleach. "Okay, I'm good, let's go."

The man started pedaling and Amber realized this was no motorized scooter. It was a trike with a really long chain made just for this purpose. It appeared to be a really good way to work out.

"So which way do I go?" the man asked. "And do you want any music?"

Amber thought about her location and the best route to her car. "Take Washington down to 1st Avenue and take a right. I'll figure it out from there. And no music, please. My head is still thumping from all the noise at the game."

"That's understandable. I'll put on a little Enya. That's calming," he said.

Amber was a bit miffed at the music, but it was relaxing, and he was working hard. He might even get a tip.

The turn at City Hall gave Amber a bearing on where she parked her car. "Go down this road here. Turn left on Adams."

The man took the turn and waited for further directions. He could tell that Amber was slightly lost, so he slowed the pace.

"Okay, Okay, I see," Amber said. "Turn right on 2nd Avenue. I'm parked closer to Monroe."

"Holy shit, you had to walk a long way!" the man yelled over his shoulder. The Enya music had gotten a bit louder.

"Yeah, it wasn't fun, that's for sure," Amber said, looking ahead to find her car, which was still half a block away.

Suddenly, the pedicab shuddered, made a terrible chunking noise, and ground to a halt.

"Well shit, that was the chain. That's okay. It happens sometimes. I got it," the man said.

He got off his seat and started walking to the rear of the pedicab.

"I think I can walk the rest from here," Amber said, facing forward, looking for her car.

"Oh, don't worry about it. I can get you there in two minutes. Plus, it's not safe in this part of town. All kinds of strange people out this time of night," the man said to her from behind with a tone of warning.

Amber did notice that there were no people in sight. At this time of night, even after a game, the business areas were deserted after 6 p.m. She sighed and started to scroll through her phone. She had a text from Misty.

"Hey, girl, let me know when you get to your car. It's a long, scary walk!!!" Misty then added the proper amount of heart emojis to make the point that she cared.

Amber sat and thought about Misty's text for a second, wondering why Misty thought she would be walking if she had hired a pedicab, until she felt a gloved hand cover her mouth and something sharp on her neck. She struggled for a second or two, but weighing 104 pounds at five-foot-nothing, it didn't last.

"You scream, and you're dead. And then Misty is next. Do you understand? If you do, nod your head. Nothing more," the man hissed into Amber's ear.

Amber nodded and was now visibly shaking.

"You know me. I'm the guy whose life you ruined!" the man said, his lips touching Amber's ear.

Amber thought for a second and tried to look around. The knife pressed tighter on her neck. She shrugged her shoulders, genuinely bewildered as to who the man was, and that enraged the man more.

"You don't even remember, do you, you bitch? You got me fired, you little shit!" He grunted, spit spraying onto her neck.

Amber shook her head to mean no and started to beg, trying to speak through the man's fingers.

"Don't you fucking try and get out of it, you bitch! It's all there. The Internet is forever. But you couldn't just stop there, could you, cunt? Now you've gotten people chasing my daughter after you doxed her, which means you've really pissed me off. If it were just me, I could let it go. At least, I thought I could let it go. But you've fucked yourself, and now you're gonna die."

The man paused for a few seconds to let that sink in, and Amber started to shake violently. She could feel her tears flow. Salt, mixed with water, mixed with fear.

Raising her chin with one finger, the murderer sliced Amber's neck from left to right, ear to ear. The blood spray formed a crimson arch, and the air filled with the smell of copper. The pulses started to die down as each one drained the life force out of Amber. Blood pooled in the plastic on the floor of the pedicab as she started the first of her death throes. Her moans and gurgling subsided. She shuddered and became limp. And with that, Amber was no more.

CHAPTER ONE

"Take a look at this fascist. This is white supremacy in the wild. Let's make him famous!"

Frankie Martinez (@FrankieGTHollywood)

PART I

Steve awoke from a fantastic nap. Not just a nap, but one of those naps where you open your eyes slowly and question what day it is. *Did I sleep until tomorrow?* he thought, with the ensuing guilt that accompanied that possibility. He had a chore list in the back of his head a mile long that fluctuated based upon how often his wife, June, mentioned any particular item.

Steve shuffled outside with garden tools in hand that he had already grabbed from the garage. It's not that he didn't like weeding, it's just that there were so many after a heavy rain that it was like plucking hairs out of his ear. Rooting out the small weeds from in between the actual plants was challenging and tedious. *Why can't we just have rocks, and I could use pool acid to sterilize the damn things?* he thought. But June loved growing things, and she could spend hours puttering in the various gardens around the house. And he loved June, so that was that.

Steve slipped on his neon yellow Crocs, thinking about how he had once been threatened with death if he wore them outside the perimeter of the yard. June had noticed him wearing them one day when he was coming home from a trip to the Pump 'N' Munch to get a bottle of malt liquor and a gyro. "How can you go out like that?" she asked. He argued that any place called Pump 'N' Munch did not have a dress code and that he fit right in with the rest of the customers. It was no use. Yellow Crocs were banned forthwith.

Steve grabbed his gear and peeped into various bedrooms to see what his prodigy was up to on his way outside. Kathy, his oldest, was finally a senior. It had been a long slog to get through high school. There had been a rather lengthy saga with a group of mean girls in the band, but a great deal of parental intervention helped resolve the issue. You'd be surprised what influence and power one can obtain when you find out the band director took liberties with club funds. Kathy was able to do private studies and take music classes at the local community college as a result, so it all worked out. The mean girls went on to find another victim.

"Is everything okay?" he asked.

Kathy sighed and flopped back on her bed. "Yeah, why wouldn't it be?" Kathy had a penchant for small amounts of passive-aggressive drama herself, but it was slowly being put under more control. Exposure to junior college students who didn't put up with that shit had really helped.

"I don't know. It's Saturday, and you are typically so cheerful on Saturdays," Steve replied as he actively thought about his future retort or a really great dad joke.

"Oh, ha ha. Don't you have some housework to do?" Kathy mused, with a perfect imitation of her mother. Steve's brain thumbed through his catalog of dad jokes and settled on an eighth-grade comeback.

"Housework? You mean that thing you are allergic to?"

Kathy looked at him with a much-practiced glare, but there was a brief smile that flickered for an instant.

"HA! I broke you!" Steve said over his shoulder, shuffling his Crocs to keep them on his feet while he plodded outside. There was no sign of his tenth-grader Brian. They had bought him an Xbox the previous year, but of course, there was a new one this year, and there was a constant subtle moaning about not having the best processor or some tech shit. Steve tried to play on it, but he just couldn't master the controllers. A desktop computer keyboard and mouse were more his speed than a console. He had become somewhat good at Battlefield as of late but couldn't do any of the spin-and-shoot-while-hopping tricks.

Steve shuffled outside and surveyed the landscape, his balding head a mixture of shiny skin, a few hairs, and sweat. They had moved into this house only recently, so there was a lot to do, with much of it tedious. Steve had just "retired" from his government job of twenty years. The added five years of his military service provided the extra time needed to retire early. "Retire" really meant taking another job at the City of Phoenix to make ends meet, but his retirement pension nicely provided funds for the house. The goal, of course, was to eventually get another pension from his new career. He was not enthused with the lower-level IT work, but he was often reminded by June that enthusiasm was not a job requirement for a government worker. She also reminded him that an idle husband who stops working too early is destined for an early death. So, naturally, Steve kept working.

Time had caught up with Steve, so even weeding slowly was work enough to make him sweat. Phoenix was often hot enough to kill most weeds between June and August, but the fall and spring temperatures brought them out in droves. A light misting would bring out weeds in such numbers that if you closed your eyes, you could hear the *hisssss* of them growing.

June was pottering about outside, planting new foliage that Steve would surely need to weed around, and she was quietly whistling some unidentifiable melody. He knew that all was right in the world if she was whistling or singing. Quietness wasn't a good sign. While June had gotten plump in her later years after the kids, she didn't consider herself fat—*fluffy* was the favorite term. Her graying hair was in a messy bun, and June flicked some stray hairs out of her face as she stood up from planting.

"What do you want for dinner tonight?" she asked. June was an amazing cook, and Steve was an amazing eater. It was a good combination that had some consequences, but nothing too serious yet. Steve was always waiting for the other shoe to drop and to be diagnosed with diabetes or another fat-related illness. Despite her being such a good cook, Steve sensed that June didn't want to face the kitchen that night.

"Hey, what's that great place we ate at that you liked?" Steve asked while he pulled up the mother of all weeds hiding under a bush. June knew this trick well, which was to get her to pick the restaurant, but she played along.

"How about Marisol's?" she asked. Steve instantly thought of deep-fried chimichangas, at least three frozen margaritas and possibly some queso. The queso at Marisol's was the next best thing to liquid crack and probably accounted for fifteen pounds hidden within Steve's gut.

"That sounds amazing! Anything you want, honey. I love your cooking, but you need a break," Steve replied, his mouth watering in anticipation of grease and tequila. "Cinco de Mayo is next week, but I'm always up for a good chimi."

When Steve served in combat in the Army before he met June, he was at prime fighting weight. Now, he was almost double that. Steve often mused that it was June's cooking at fault. Being on the short side, it occurred to him that he was just over 50, and being fatter just came with the territory.

"Why don't you take off your very fashionable shoes and your awesome shorts and get dressed?" June suggested.

June always had a way of keeping Steve in check when it came to fashion. Apparently, nine-year-old gym shorts were not in fashion anymore, even with a KISS t-shirt. They were the type of gym shorts that, if worn properly, presented a free-flowing airspace in your nether regions but also, on occasion, exposed the family jewels in a manner unbecoming to a 50-year-old man.

Steve slipped out of his Crocs and shorts, tripping on the way out of the bedroom with the shorts entangling his legs. He wasn't as limber as he used to be. June was constantly trying to get him to try yoga or at least some form of stretching.

Steve completed the redundant task of undressing and redressing and finding his Sketchers, which was always a chore in and of itself. June was finishing up straightening the kitchen while Steve searched for the kids.

"KATHY… BRIAN!" Steve yelled up the stairs. No reply. "HELLO?" he puffed as he started walking up what seemed like an endless flight of stairs. The house was taller than it was wide, and thankfully, the master bedroom was on the bottom floor. He reached the top of the stairs as Kathy came out, seemingly ready for a medieval ball. She was still in that mostly black phase with long, flowing, and wavy hair that was now silvery gray. However, she was on the mend from being a goth and was adding some red and yellow to her repertoire. That could still change at any time.

"Are we leaving?" Kathy asked with a bit of "why didn't we leave 30 minutes ago and why wasn't I notified we were about to leave?" tone.

"We can leave if you're ready. I was waiting for you. Hey, you're wearing something new! Yoga pants!" Steve quipped. His dad joke solicited an almost imperceptible eye roll. Kathy wore varying forms of yoga pants almost every day. But, in spite of the joke, her eye rolls were much less obvious now that June had smacked her verbally for about a year until the unconscious and instantaneous urge to pull her eyes to the back of her skull subsided.

Steve shuffled down to Brian's room. He could have done it blindfolded and just followed the smell. While Steve couldn't remember if he smelled like sweaty socks dipped in urine at Brian's age, he was assured by June that he did and that it was normal. Steve and June had dated since they were fifteen, and June was an old soul. From her point of view, she was raising one more fifteen-year-old. Regardless, Steve had to mainly breathe through pursed lips when approaching the closed door. He marveled at how the smell wafted under the door. Perhaps some foam insulation might be in order.

Steve knocked and gently cracked the door after waiting for the mandatory thirty seconds. One never really knew what happened behind his door, nor did one want to. Steve held back from the door and waited, trying hard not to listen to any sounds that came forth from Brian's room. Some things heard cannot be unheard. The agreed-upon time elapsed, and Steve slowly opened the door to an invisible spiral of funk.

Brian was oblivious to the world, with noise-cancelling headphones amplifying the chaos of Call of Duty, a version God knows. There was always a new Call of Duty to buy. Soldiers in the Future, World War II, World War I, Cold War, Special Ops, and for all Steve knew, there was a new edition for the War of 1812 coming out for Christmas.

Brian continued to mercilessly kill his multiplayer combatants unabated as he finished off another 100-calorie pack of Ritz Peanut Butter Crackers. Many of the other fallen packages littered the floor around the trashcan. His sister had mentioned that he was eating 1200 calories in 100-calorie packs a day, which may have accounted for a bit of weight gain. Of course, she mentioned it in the worst possible way, which caused about a week of eye-rolling hell. His weight, combined with his dark, greasy hair and scraggy and patchy beard, gave him the stereotypical look of a seasoned gamer. A look that Steve and June chipped away at as they drew him away from his games at every opportunity for true human interaction.

Steve slowly came to the side of Brian, waving frantically while trying to step over the other 11 Ritz packages and various socks. Brian jumped when Steve finally got into his peripheral vision, and a "shit" came out as a reflex. Steve wasn't bothered by the more mundane curse words unless they were tossed at an individual. Even the word "stupid" wasn't allowed.

"Why didn't you knock?" Brian shouted, his headphones still vomiting the sounds of a massive digital battle and his long and fairly greasy brown hair covering his eyes. Steve wondered on more than one occasion how he could see past his mop.

Steve pretended to talk and mouthed meaningless words until Brian took off his headphones. The noise of war was at about 150 decibels, which is what Steve imagined the actual war would be at.

"I did. But your constant dying in battle prevented you from hearing me. Don't you ever dodge?" Steve said, knowing that his own battle skills hobbled him, even though he had done the real thing while in the Army. To compensate, Steve was a fan of falling on the ground in a prone position, as the CTRL key was pretty easy to hit in an emergency. It was like dodging in a way, wasn't it?

"It's from you. I LEARNED IT ALL FROM YOU!" Brian shouted. Steve was quite proud that he had done his job well enough that Brian knew of the old "don't do drugs" commercials.

"Well, let's go. Waiting for you now. Let's eat."

Brian jumped up, but only after carefully exiting the game so as not to let his avatar get killed over and over. They walked out together and clomped down the stairs. While Steve was not wearing his Crocs, Brian did seem to have ridiculously large shoes. They inevitably clumped wherever he went. And, of course, they smelled like rotting death.

Brian ushered his pride out of the house and locked up. There were several locks, as one can never have too many locks. Next came the alarm. There was always a double-check at some point where Steve would ask, "Did anyone alarm?" Smartphones are amazing, and like magic, the fortress was protected from at least a walk-by criminal. A true cat burglar would come in through the roof, Steve mused. While the Phoenix area had its fair share of crime, cat burglars were in short supply and didn't often target moderately standard housing like theirs. At least, that is what he told himself.

PART II

Marisol's was a nice, family-friendly Mexican restaurant and one of about twenty thousand in the area. There was TexMex, CalMex, New Mexican, Sonoran, and dozens of other subregional areas that called Mexican food their own. Marisol's was one of the family favorites. It was not a chain but had several in town, each with its own following. Steve gathered that a different sibling of the same family ran each one as each had their own culture, even though they mostly shared the same menu. Steve wondered how many children Marisol had or even if there was a Marisol. It was something to ponder over a margarita.

As usual for a Saturday night, there was a wait. On some nights, the wait could be half an hour or more. June went to put her name on the list. Actually, she put Steve's name on the list. It's just what she did.

"The wait is about twenty," June said.

"Well, that's not bad. Wait until next week. You do want to come back next week for Cinco de Mayo, don't you?" Steve asked.

June paused. "I don't like the crowds. It reminds me of Mother's Day, too many kids and stressed-out moms. But if you really want to, we can." When she said this, she gave Steve the impression that what she meant was *I don't want to cook, so yes.* So, Steve went with that. Plus, he wanted a margarita.

"Anything you want, honey," Steve said. "I'll see if I can make a reservation."

"You know they don't take reservations. They don't even allow you to call ahead," June said.

"Well, I suppose we will just come early then," Steve said in earnest to cement into place the plan and secure a future margarita. Marisol's did make a good and consistent frozen margarita.

June nodded, and then she joined Brian and Kathy in studying their smartphones and waited. June typically scrolled down her Instagram feed. It was filled with various food channels and dog videos. Steve wondered what you called someone's channel on Instagram. Their account? Channel? Stream? It was a bit of a mystery.

The kids each had their own sites and social media feeds, and Steve and June made it known that some things were off-limits until college. Porn and some of the other seedier parts of the Internet were just a no-go. Occasional checks and some crafty Wi-Fi monitoring typically kept the specter of oversight ever-present. Still, Steve did worry about the unfettered chatter of social media. Steve had his own Instagram account filled with typical man stuff. Some workout channels (or were they accounts?) and an occasional boob mixed with various science fiction topics. He had an OpenBook account used exclusively to connect with a few old high school friends, his mom, and the local neighborhood organization. That had really come in handy during the last storm, with neighbors helping neighbors. Other than that, Steve rarely posted anything. He didn't think most of his life was that interesting, much less worthy for others to stalk.

The hostess finally called Steve's name, and they were taken to their booth, Brian *clop-clopping* in the rear. While not all booths were created equal, the ones at Marisol's were spacious. Steve truly hated sitting in a booth that was made for a 32-inch waist. On more than one occasion, when the booth was already tight, the addition of a bit of food almost caused the need for a pry bar and some Vaseline to ooze out of the seat.

Steve was happy to see that they got a seat with their favorite server. She was a motherly Hispanic woman with round arms and comfortable shoes to compensate for the hours she spent on her feet. She was the type of waitress who seemed to instinctively know what you needed, and if you had her more than once, she remembered absolutely everything. It was somewhat savant in nature, but she seemed to have been doing this for a long time for both Marisol's and her own family. She was no doubt also an excellent cook herself. Sadly, Steve had forgotten her name again.

"Heeeeeyyyyyy, Mr. and Mrs. Richardson! How are you guys?" she beamed. She always seemed to be genuinely happy to see their family. They always tipped exceptionally well, but this didn't seem to matter, at least not on the outside.

"Hey, Veronica, we're doing great! How are you?" June asked with an equal amount of genuine concern.

"Veronica. Her name is Veronica," Steve mumbled to himself. He knew a Veronica and a Selma, who typically served them, but he was horrible with names and faces.

"Doing great, doing great. Iced tea and a frozen?" Veronica asked.

"Absolutely!" Steve beamed and started to dive in on the chips and salsa Veronica had brought to the table. Marisol's had literally the best chips and salsa in the area, in addition to the crack-laced queso. The chips were the flour-tortilla kind that was freshly deep-fried and glistening with grease and salt crystals. The salsa was simply ground-up jalapeños and tomatoes and a mix of who-knows-what, all blended into a thick paste. Steve had often called it "los dos calientes," as it burned going in as much as it burned coming out four hours later. But it was so damn addictive.

"What will y'all have?" Veronica asked Brian and Kathy.

Kathy pulled her eyes away from her phone. "I'll just have water," she replied.

Brian mumbled something incoherent until June physically stomped on his toe in his clown shoes. Steve was convinced he could both hear and smell the puff of mold come out.

"I'll also have water, thank you," Brian said in a much clearer voice. Both children had been taught manners to strangers and employees alike. You could always tell a person's character by how they treated the people who served them food. June had been a food server when she was thirteen when she worked illegally to support her family at a local Bonanza. It was a cheap steak restaurant owned by a man named Farad. He liked to employ illegal aliens or undocumented workers, depending upon your affiliation. He also liked underage girls to entice the local college students. Fortunately, June avoided everything other than a few attempted gropes from drunken frats.

"Do you know what you'll want to eat? Queso?" Veronica asked, already knowing what the answers would be.

"Oh yesssssss," Steve hissed with wide eyes like a true crack addict…pupils all dilated.

Veronica smirked. She never got tired of Steve's responses. Most customers were a bit cranky, but this family was very kind. "And so, what else then?"

June and Steve ordered their usuals: ground beef chimichanga for Steve and chicken flautas for June. The kids ordered tacos and a quesadilla to share. Marisol's made a great quesadilla with an unusual amount of onion and peppers—just enough to make it a meal.

Steve and June bantered while Kathy and Brian occasionally engaged in a topic they found interesting—at least more interesting than the latest makeup tutorial. Two baskets of chips and a scraped-clean queso bowl later, their meal arrived.

Steve did his standard bit and took the whole jalapeño from his literally sizzling hot plate of chimi and cheese goodness and made it dance across his plate. "Ay, ay, ay!" Steve mimicked. Unbeknownst to the children, this was almost a perfect imitation of an old Warner Bros cartoon where the Mexican chili pepper hops across the blazing desert. Oddly, Steve had a memory that functions in such a way that he could not remember names but could recite lines and scenes from any movie, TV show, or song he had ever heard. This became an issue when trying to relate to anyone under forty. The time at work when Steve exclaimed, "We're screwed, man! We're fucked! We're doomed!" when a server went down was met with a bit of alarm. "You know, *Aliens?* Bill Paxton?" Steve said, as he tried to recover from what could have been a true HR issue. But, after several years working at the City of Phoenix, and after passing probation once again, Steve tried to keep the jokes to 2005 or later.

Veronica did her best to keep up with the margarita refills. She was a seasoned server who knew if she kept asking Steve, "One more?" he may still say yes. So Veronica asked, "One more?"

"Oh yeah, keep 'em coming, keep 'em coming!" Steve belted with an almost perfect imitation of Randy Quaid on *Independence Day*. Of course, Randy was talking about coffee, but a margarita would have been more appropriate.

Veronica smiled. Once again, as a skilled server, she added up the extra cost of the margarita in her tip, as she also knew that June was a great tipper.

The final three margaritas were served and the check appeared after a quick nod from June when asked if she was ready to settle up. June knew that if they lingered any longer, the kids would dissolve into lumps, and Steve would have a fourth margarita.

With the check paid, Steve, June, and the children easily slipped out of the spacious booths. Again, Steve was truly grateful for the depth of Marisol's booths. They shuffled to the car, visibly fuller and slower than when they came in.

"What do you want to do for the rest of the evening? Ice cream?" Steve asked June.

"Oh, we don't need ice cream. We just ate," June said.

"That's the best time for ice cream!" Steve pushed with a fervent need in his moderately drunken state to have some Cold Stone Creamery Peanut Butter Deluxe ice cream. It was only 1800 calories, but who was counting? Marisol's booth still had plenty of room left.

As June was driving, the decision was made to keep on driving and not succumb to the calorie-laden deliciousness. Steve sat and watched the world go by as he longed for ice cream. The kids sat in the back. A subtle blue light from their phones caused the car to glow like a light cycle from *Tron*. At least, that is what Steve imagined.

PART III

Sunday went as expected—lazing in bed and a good lunch and some routine chores—and like magic, it was Monday. The week progressed in a standard and normal momentum. Sunday was a quantum physics conundrum where space/time caused a perception gap between the hours of 1 p.m. to 5 p.m. The time between those four hours simply disappeared.

Steve walked into his cubicle in the squat City Hall building. It was just as he had left it, with papers scattered about, books for certifications he had yet to study for, and a coffee cup from the Starbucks down the street.

Steve booted up his computer. He always shut down his computer at the end of each day as, once upon a time, for whatever reason, a flag was thrown that there was a hacking attempt coming from his computer. Nothing came of it, and Steve had no idea what had happened. The main IT department still commandeered his computer and went through it on a genetic level before giving it back. Not one to repeat a stressful situation, Steve powered down each day. This also allowed him a few minutes to brace for the day while his system booted up in the morning.

Most days were quite boring. Steve had spent twenty-plus years at the City of Peoria and five in the Army. Over those careers, he began to truly see the complete stupidity of most people. In IT, he had worked his way up from a computer tech to a manager and saw the same issues being repeated over two decades of technological upgrades. It was painful. For the last few years at Peoria, he fortunately had staff that kept human-to-human contact with the outside world to a minimum. It's not that Steve didn't like people. It's just that they were so damn irritating.

Now Steve was back to square one. To retire on time and at the first available instant to collect his first pension, he took the first decent government job to come along that would provide another one. Double-dipping was the usual term, and June was quite vocal that Steve could just not retire. "It will kill you," she often said. Being desktop support again wasn't hard. It was just boring, but it paid well and kept Steve in the office and June happy. Between his salary and pension, he was making more money than ever. Plus, double-dipping another pension in five more years or so wouldn't hurt when he started to collect Social Security and actually retire. But damn those needy people.

"Hey, what's up, man?" Rick, his coworker, said as he groundhogged over the cubicle wall. Or was it prairie dogging? Regardless, Rick always had a way of popping up and peeping over. Steve's first thought was that he was usually just trying to see what was on Steve's screen until a handy-dandy privacy screen was installed that made peeping impossible, so he knew that wasn't the reason for Rick's attention. Plus, reading the Drudge Report was one of Steve's obsessions and filled in the time between needy people. The privacy screen also helped to conceal his habit.

"Hey, Rick," Steve said without looking up. "What's up with you?" It's not that Steve didn't care, but Rick was a mixtape on repeat—a smattering of conspiracy theories, obscure occult facts, and a predilection for the most fantastical political theories. The more unbelievable, the better. Steve was pretty sure that even at thirty-five, Rick was a virgin. He was still fun to work around and was a real computer whiz, but you could only put up with him in small doses. Unfortunately, even a lunch with Rick was enough for a week of normal conversation.

"Hey, same shit, different day, man. Have you checked your email yet?" Rick asked.

"No, not yet, I'm still rebooting," Steve lied, hoping to fool Rick into believing he was hard at work and not surfing the Web. Steve was a hard worker but found that checking email meant getting a support ticket, and it was just too damn early to reset another user's password.

Rick blurted in his typical fashion, "We've got to take this bullshit class. It's mandatory, man. MANDATORY! So you know it's bullshit."

Steve pondered this bait and gave his most concerned yet deeply unconcerned scowl. "What is this bullshit you speaketh of, Rick? Why art thou so perturbed?" Steve said in his worst Ye Olde English accent. In his head, visions of *The Princess Bride* flashed by as he formulated his next quote reply.

"It's that PC bullshit where we all get to talk about how we feel about being white and shit like that! It's bullshit!" Rick started to hiss the last few words when he realized that Director Garcia had left her office and was walking down the hall towards them. Rose Garcia had worked her way up in the public works department and was genial in general but had a true mean streak at times. Steve got along with her, but Rick got along with hardly anyone.

"Bullshit. You keep using that word. I do not think it means what you think it means." Steve smiled at popping in a *Princess Bride* quote, even though Rick had no idea what it meant. Again, this was the real challenge when talking to anyone younger than forty.

"You're a turd, Steve. Of course, I know what it means. It's bullshit, and I can smell bullshit when I smell it," Rick said, scowling. "First, the class, and then I get shitcanned to make space for who-knows-what-people-of-color or some other shit!"

Steve thought that Rick saying that he could smell bullshit when he smelled bullshit seemed a bit obvious. But then again, Rick wasn't the most articulate person.

Steve changed the topic as Rose got closer. He asked Rick about the next upgrade cycle to quickly change the topic from bitching back to work.

"Good morning, gentlemen," Rose said as she strolled along with her coffee cup and soft leather briefcase.

"Good morning, ma'am," Steve replied as she passed and bugged his eyes out at Rick to do the same.

"Hey, good morning!" Rick shouted in an oddly raised voice as he made an innocuous social greeting into an awkward cluster-fuck of an interaction.

Rose looked behind her and studied Rick's face for a moment, and she quickly realized that the man-child was just an odd egg and moved on. There were a few odd folks in the department, as being odd wasn't a fireable offense yet. In fact, there were so few fireable offenses that eventually, a better part of anyone who stayed for longer than five years was an odd egg. It was that fact that allowed Steve to crack an occasional joke that skirted the limits of HR yet still kept his coworkers amused. In the private sector, Steve would have lasted a month. Rick would have lasted a day. Besides, to quote *Ghostbusters*, "in the private sector, they expect results."

Rick continued to stare at Rose as she walked away. Of course, it was a little too leering and a little too long, so Steve pretended not to notice any longer and went back to watching his computer boot up. He had secretly turned it off to have it boot up again, just to bide time for Rick to get bored and go away. Unfortunately, Rick was never bored.

"Do you think she likes men?" Rick asked, still watching Rose walk down the hallway.

Steve shrugged and murmured, "I don't really know, Rick. Why don't you ask her?"

Rick contemplated this for a moment until Rose went into her office. "Maybe I will, Steve. Maybe I will. You know, I do like those Latinas," Rick pondered this a bit more and wandered away. Steve continued to watch his computer boot up while he wondered just how he had wound up working with someone like Rick.

PART IV

It was Friday, and everyone in the office was in casual clothes. For Steve, this meant jeans and his usual Polo shirt. For Rick, this meant dirty jeans and a typically inappropriate t-shirt. This week, it was a Def Leopard concert shirt, complete with "Pour some sugar on me" graphics. It was really the most inappropriate shirt to wear when attending a mandatory all-staff meeting.

"Hey, douchebag!" Rick blurted while Steve pretended that he wasn't talking to him. It was easy to do, as Rick just tended to speak to people in general without actually looking at anybody.

Michelle, the accountant from down the hall, was sitting at the same round table in a sea of identical round tables and immediately regretted her seating choice. She glared harshly at Steve. Steve thought and acted quickly. "Rick, don't call yourself that. It's rude."

Rick rolled his eyes. "Whatever, man. I'm just joshin'."

The rest of the staff slowly strolled in and signed their names at a large table with muffins and juice. It was a morning meeting, after all, and the accounting section was in charge of snacks. They were mostly plump women, and while that shouldn't mean anything, it still did. They got some really great muffins, as they truly appreciated a great muffin.

Steve picked at a really plump bran muffin and sipped some orange juice. He noted Michelle had cut a muffin in half and left the other half at the table. *Who in hell would eat the other half of the muffin?* Steve thought as he pinched another raisin out of his. Michelle was one to really let you know her opinion in a passive-aggressive way. And sometimes in an aggressive-aggressive way. It depended upon the receiver, and she rotated between who she liked and who she didn't like. It didn't help that she was once one of those plump accountants who then had a stomach staple procedure. She went from plump to somewhat saggy, but she had purchased all new clothes to hold it all in. In the end, she got smaller but a lot meaner. "Wow, when you lost weight, you really became a bitch!" she was told by Joyce, the accountant, who promptly retired a month later.

After the chit-chat and muffin extravaganza died down, Rose took the podium and waited for a solid fifteen seconds before everyone noticed and quieted down.

Rose leaned into the microphone. "Hello, all. I appreciate you coming down here today. We've come a long way as an organization, and I really want to say thank you to each and every one of you for the great job you've been doing since I arrived here two years ago this week."

A golf clap went through the crowd. All except for Rick, who applauded in an exaggerated imitation of a pelican flying. "Whooot!" Rick yelled.

Rose scanned the crowd and made note. The pain of embarrassment from Director Garcia would need to be more severe for Rick, and Steve knew it. Michelle edged further away and concentrated on her half-muffin.

"We all know that more can be done and that we can all improve. Even Rick," Rose continued. "With that, I'd like to introduce Joy Sanchez from human resources."

Joy stood up from her chair beside the podium and gave her assistant the thumb drive with her presentation on it. Steve wondered why they hadn't prepared the presentation before. But then again, they were from HR.

"Thank you, Director Garcia. I'm so glad you invited me today." Joy stalled as her assistant went through the tasks of finding the presentation and loading it up. Steve quickly scanned the other titles on the jump drive. Everything was there, from sex discrimination, microaggressions, race and the law to LGBTQ acceptance. *I'll bet she's fun at parties*, Steve thought as the assistant finally loaded the correct presentation.

Joy was handed the remote control and pointer and began her presentation while her assistant recovered in the chair next to her, obviously flustered.

"Director Garcia has brought us here today to discuss critical race theory. Here at the City, we really think about it as making things right through listening to others," Joy beamed. This was the first of many courses and Joy loved each and every one. It was her passion.

Rick acted as if he had smelled a ripe fart and loudly banged his head on the table, but Joy was a professional and kept on with the presentation. The audience sat through the thirty slides and forty-five minutes of canned dialogue with the patience that only a civil servant has. Many grocery lists were made, and holiday plans were mulled over. But at the end, another smattering of golf claps was had, and the mandatory training was over for the year. It was a rite of passage.

Then came the question-and-answer part of the program. There was always a Q&A session, and for the most part, they were silent. For the most part—until today.

Steve continued to stare at his feet as he heard the shuffling of a few hands being raised. The rustle of clothes meant that the forty-five-minute presentation would continue unabated until everyone got the note to just shut up so it would end. It was the unwritten civil service rule: thou shalt not make comments nor ask questions. Steve was surprised to hear another voice that wasn't Rick.

A younger-looking man-boy with horn-rimmed glasses and skinny jeans started to emote. "So if we're all inherently racist, and it's been this way for a long time, that means it's systemic. So, if it's systemic already, wouldn't that mean the same people who are making us take this course are the same people who are, in fact, racist? Why don't they just take the course and leave the rest of us alone?"

Steve pondered on this and about the swift retribution that would follow.

"The point of this training is to make us all better listeners and to understand different points of view," Rose said, scowling faintly and burning the face of the nameless hipster into her brain for future reference.

"Well, what if we are already good listeners?" the hipster replied, arms folded and a clear smirk on his face. He was making the original sin of trying to be a smart ass to the director in public.

Rose glanced at the supervisor of the soon-to-be reassigned non-person next to him. He was squirming with folded hands and a downward stare, knowing what he would be forced to do later to mitigate the insolence. It was well known that Director Garcia was not one for joking and didn't really understand most humor in general. Her five-second glance was noticed by everyone paying attention, and the rest of the hands went down as quickly as they had risen.

"Do we have any more questions?" Rose asked rhetorically.

Steve listened for a response as he studied the cracks in the circular wooden table. A solid count to three, and they were done.

"Well, let us give Joy a round of applause! Thank you, Joy, for joining us today to kick off this important program!" Rose beamed as she started the golf clap in an overexaggerated way.

Rose continued to clap and the rest of the employees, at least the ones still awake, followed suit, Rick leading the same way as he began with flapping claps. Rose glared in his direction again, and another brand of Rick's face was seared into her brain, next to the hipster.

The crowd shuffled to the exit, scooping up any remaining muffins and drinks, except for the half muffin that Michelle left. Steve stayed behind to help clean up. Helping clean up meant he didn't need to reboot his computer for now. Plus, the folks from accounting were geeky but nice, and they had awesome potlucks that Steve was invited to. Not many people from IT were invited to the accounting potluck, so it was a big deal. Plus, Steve really liked those tiny hot dogs in BBQ sauce that Sally, the accountant, brought in.

Steve eventually wandered back across the street from the HR building to City Hall and up to his cubicle. Most of the other staff were back in their individual spaces, getting ready to pretend to consider getting back to work. Michelle wandered by, and prairie dogged over Steve's cubicle wall. Or was it a meerkat? Was she meerkatting?

"What do you think Rick meant today?" she asked.

Steve looked blankly back at Michelle, knowing he was being baited into responding to something that only Michelle perceived.

"I'm not sure. What do you think he meant?" Steve asked. He knew that if he kept answering questions with questions, she would eventually answer herself. It was a fun but exhausting game. Plus, you never knew what Michelle thought, just like you never knew why she only ate half a muffin, sacrificing the other half to uneaten oblivion.

"I think he was calling me a douche. I'm pretty sure of it," Michelle replied, thereby rewriting history in her head.

Steve was sure that Rick was calling him a douche, but to contradict Michelle was to ensure that she would go to someone else about you with another imaginary slight fabricated solely in her need to be wronged in some way. It made talking with her a thought exercise.

"I don't know. Do you think he did?" Steve asked, playing the game a bit longer. He could do this forever.

"I think I need to complain this time. I mean, he said it in front of everybody. Even you heard it!" Michelle emoted with watery eyes.

Steve thought about what question to ask her next when Rick started to come down the hallway, loudly saying hello to every cubicle he passed while peering at their computer screens. His penchant for blurting out what you were looking at on your screen was widely known. Lord help you if you were on a website that could even remotely be considered suggestively improper. It was like chum to sharks.

"Hey, Carla! Looking at men in bathing suits again?" Rick blurted as he announced his presence.

Michelle shrunk below cube height and scurried away as dozens of Steve's coworkers hit the Windows and L keys to lock their screens until the shark passed. It was best to remain motionless to avoid capturing Rick's attention. The best defense was to look boring.

Rick came up to Steve's cube and peeped inside.

"Hey, douche. What did you think of the training?" Rick said with exaggerated finger air quotes.

Steve automatically started to reboot his computer. "It was okay, I guess. I just want to get it finished and get credit for it. It's the same as any other training we have to take."

"Bullshit, like hell it is!" Rick blurted. "It's fucking brainwashing commie shit!"

Steve winced. It was times like this that even being in the vicinity of Rick was like being in the blast radius of a hand grenade. You were bound to be a casualty.

"Dude, lower your voice," Steve hissed. "Don't get me in trouble. I'm not joking."

Rick scowled. "Dude, don't be a pansy. I know it's bullshit. You know it's bullshit! Just call it bullshit!"

"I don't care if it's bullshit. Most of our training is bullshit. I just want to do it and be done with it. I don't have to agree with it. I don't care either way! My computer is almost booted up, and

I've got to finish up for the day," Steve said as he turned to face his monitor.

"Whatever, douchebag. Happy Friday," Rick replied as he stomped away. When Rick stomped, it was an overexaggerated stomp that a teenager would do, complete with mumbling under his breath along the way.

Steve sighed and stared at his login screen for a good five minutes before logging in for the last time. His email popup told him that the promised class link was there. Steve clicked on the link and signed up for the absolute last date for the class in late July and logged out for the weekend with another extended sigh.

PART V

Steve awoke on Saturday morning with some reluctance, as it was yard work day. The heat had already started, and it was only nine.

"I'm going to the bathroom," Steve told June. Picking up his phone, he sauntered into the bathroom for the morning tradition of reviewing the news and other events that may have happened overnight. He shuffled and dropped his shorts and underwear on the floor and tripped on them.

"Fuck me!" Steve muttered as he stopped himself from falling into the toilet. June snickered and rolled her eyes imperceptibly at the sounds coming from the bathroom. She knew that Steve would be in there for no fewer than twenty minutes.

Steve scrolled through his bookmarks and reviewed the news of the day. He followed several news sites for a variety of what was important enough to be reported. He could always tell when a new book or movie was about to be released from the incessant stories on whatever actor was featured for eating ice cream or lamenting their troubled childhood.

After one too many stories on Robert Downy Jr., he flipped to some of the more obscure media websites. Most of the time, they featured a mix of conspiracy theories and fringe news, but on occasion, Steve would pick up a nugget that would later actually hit some of the mainstream media. He prided himself on seeing patterns and on prognosticating the future. He was, in his own mind, a modern-day Nostradamus.

The trend of the moment was on that cursed critical race theory and all that is evil about it. Truly, after the events of the previous week, Steve had more than he wanted on the topic and just wished it would all go away. He hated being lectured on how he should feel, what he should be guilty about, or how to fret more strenuously to atone for some past transgression centuries ago.

The obligatory twenty minutes passed, and Steve finished up. The actual bathroom process had only taken a few minutes, but you never knew if there were more up in there waiting. Best read the news to make sure while you wait.

As he walked slowly down the hall from his bedroom, he noted the noises from his children's rooms, or more accurately, the lack of noises. What joy it must be to sleep past ten on Saturday. Brian and Kathy would probably be ghosts until well after lunch.

June whistled a tune from the kitchen as she cooked a light breakfast. Steve and the kids knew if Mom was singing or whistling, all was right in the world.

The smell of beef belly bacon and eggs filled the house with a greasy smoke that could cause even a vegan to salivate. There was something about beef bacon that was truly delicious. Sadly, June was allergic to pork due to the penicillin used to inoculate pigs.

Somehow, it stayed in the pig and was passed on with a disgustingly violent reaction when it reached June's gut. So, beef bacon it was, and it was indeed good. Steve would routinely joke that since pigs were biologically very similar to humans, when Armageddon came about, she wouldn't be able to eat anyone. June would do a polite "ha ha" and shake her head. She only heard that joke about once a month.

Steve and June sat down at the kitchen table to eat. "What do you want to do today?" Steve asked with the clear hope it was something fun.

"I guess we should do yard work so we can relax tomorrow. Remember that tomorrow is Cinco de Mayo," June said.

Steve suddenly remembered that while tomorrow may be Cinco de Mayo, today was Star Wars Day.

"Oh, hey! May the Fourth be with you!" Steve exclaimed proudly. June again rolled her eyes in a counterclockwise direction this time and took a sip of her coffee. She had also heard this one annually since Star Wars Day became a thing.

"I am one with the Force, and the Force is with me," June said with a sly smile. Steve beamed that she had actually paid close enough attention to *Rogue One* to remember that line. It was a great success.

"I am one with the Force, and the Force is with me!" Steve rejoined before chowing down on some beef bacon. Again, it was amazing.

Once the plates were cleaned of their bounty, June cleaned the table, and Steve bagged up the trash to take outside. The time had come to do the deed of yard work. Steve put on his yellow Crocs and headed through the garage to the trashcans. He wondered if he could get away with just trimming the edges of the lawn instead of a full yard mow. It hadn't rained much lately, and grass tended to grow more slowly until the rains picked up again. It being Arizona, most everything died in the summer unless artificially propped up by daily watering.

After a brief survey and approval from June, it was determined that the mowing could wait a week—Another small victory for Steve and more progress toward his goal of getting a nap later.

June started her thing, which was mainly gardening. She routinely planted and dug up a huge variety of plants as they went through their desert life cycle. She was at peak happiness when she was gardening. June whistled as usual and wiggled her toes in the dirt. She had a tendency to rip off toenails due to her refusal to wear shoes while working. Steve had bought her some blue Crocs, and they generally sat in the closet.

"What are you planting this time?" Steve shouted to June over the hum of the electric weed whacker.

"Some more ground cover plants to hold in some of the dirt moisture," June replied as she dug another hole.

"I'm pretty sure those black moth things are laying eggs in the grape vine again," June said sadly. Those eggs popped out cute caterpillars that would eat each and every leaf of the vine if allowed to go unchecked.

"I think I need to pull out the Pam or canola spray now," June said defiantly. Oil was pretty effective at violently suffocating eggs and emerging caterpillars. It also allowed you to eat any surviving grapes later. Or at least the ones that the birds didn't get. June did love the grapes.

Steve finished up the strimming and put the tools away just as June finished her planting. Steve waited with bated breath as he observed June. *Was she going to sit down? Did she have another chore?* The guilt of stopping work before June was unbearable. His questions were soon answered when June sat down and pulled out two bottles of water she had put in a small cooler. She always did plan ahead, and Steve was grateful. He was also relieved that there might still be time for a nap.

"Whew, that was good work!" Steve said as he drank the entire bottle of water. He hoped that she would agree.

"Yes, it was. I'm very happy about how the lantana is doing. I was worried it wouldn't take," June said. The lantana had not only taken well to the soil but there were lantana babies sprouting at the corners of the fence. They had become entangled with the cat claws that had climbed the block wall fence. The cat claws had literally taken the lantana up the wall. It made for a pretty yard, and June approved.

Steve and June decided to take a dip in the pool to cool off. It was early afternoon and over a hundred and ten degrees. The sun was brutal, but June had strategically arranged several awnings to maximize the shade.

Kathy opened her window, which was above the pool. "Hey, you guys—don't make me sick!" Kathy said, interrupting a kiss between her parents.

"Hey, don't cool the desert!" Steve retorted. It was a constant battle to keep the cold air inside the house where it belonged and the oppressive heat outside. Since the kids didn't pay their own electricity bills, they didn't have any concept of a shut window or door.

Kathy grunted and rolled her eyes. Steve began to wonder if that was a learned skill or a genetic trait. "Well, that worked," Steve said as he leaned in to kiss June again, hoping that would force his daughter's retreat and keep the cool air in the house.

There was an instant chill as June and Steve walked back into the house and air conditioning. The rate of evaporation this time of year was extreme, and after enduring the heat, the intense chill of a wet bathing suit was bracing.

Brian was in the kitchen watching his parents scramble to the bedroom. He was just waking up and poured a ramen bowl-sized serving of cereal. The TV was tuned to some type of Japanese game show where they take turns hitting each other in the crotch. It was educational.

"You guys are so weird," Brian mumbled after his parents as he noisily slurped his cereal between screams of anguish from the television.

June went into the bedroom and closed the door. She raced to the shower and got warm. Steve took off his clinging icy suit and UV shirt. That shirt was truly ugly, being bright yellow, but it kept the sun off his arms and back. It wasn't an outfit to wear in public.

June finished up, and Steve stepped into a still-running shower. After a flash of searing pain that he reprimanded himself for not anticipating, he turned down the hot water to a human level and showered off.

Steve turned off the shower and dried off. He stepped into the cool bedroom and collapsed on the bed. June was already there with her towel. Steve felt that spark of blood rush into key places, so he flopped his towel open and lay spread-legged on the bed.

"How can you resist that?" Steve beamed while looking away slyly. It was a subtle thing but effective.

June rolled her eyes and said, "Well, I don't see how I can. I'm helpless."

Again, Steve wondered about the genetic eye-rolling thing, but it soon passed as June and Steve had some mommy-daddy time before a much-needed nap.

PART VI

It was finally Cinco de Mayo, or really the "Revenge of the Fifth," as Steve liked to call it. There was a Star Wars reference for practically every occasion, and the worse, the better. In the end, when the puns got too bad to tolerate, there was always "I find your lack of faith disturbing." It was the little things that counted.

Steve slept in until, well, who knows? Was it ten? June had already gotten up and was bustling in the kitchen. Steve could hear the rattling of silverware, and the smell of more beef bacon filled the house.

Oh, maybe she will bring me breakfast in bed! Steve thought and pretended to sleep.

Sure enough, June came in with two plates of bacon, cheesy eggs, and toast. June's cheesy eggs were amazing, with the perfect amount of American cheese blended into scrambled eggs. And these weren't just any ordinary eggs. They were from free-range, grass and bug-fed chickens from somebody's farm. This anonymous somebody sold the eggs a few miles away at a full-time farmer's market. The yolks were somewhat orange and not yellow. They cooked completely differently than store-bought eggs. The drive to the market was so worth it.

"Well, this is a pleasant surprise!" Steve exclaimed as he sat up in bed. He started searching for the Apple TV remote. June always wanted to watch some home improvement or cooking show on Sunday morning, and while there were Star Wars movies to watch since it was a Sith holiday, Steve rewarded June with some random farm cooking show.

June knew that Steve was being gracious, as she brought breakfast in bed almost every Sunday anyway. It made her feel appreciated just the same.

Steve and June ate the juicy eggs on top of the jellied toast and watched how to make true Southern deviled eggs. Truth be told, June's deviled eggs were the best, and even better when she could get a hold of those damn eggs. Steve thought it was ironic that they were eating eggs while watching a random show about eggs.

"What do you want to do today?" Steve asked June.

"I don't know. What do you want to do?" June replied with a question in between bacon bites.

"I don't know. What do you want to do?" Steve retorted.

June knew that Steve could keep this up for several minutes and broke the Groundhog Day cycle, as amusing as it was. Sometimes.

"We're eating out tonight at Marisol's for Cinco de Mayo. We could always take the kids to see a movie, I guess. We haven't seen a movie in an actual movie theater for a long time."

Steve pondered this. "What movies are out?"

June tapped her phone alive and started to search for a good movie. "We could always go see that new superhero movie," June said.

Steve pondered this as well. June was referring to a knock-off superhero flick that was a campy redo of a mishmash of the latest Marvel and DC movies. It got terrible reviews, and Steve had secretly hoped that there was another movie that wasn't so incurably stupid as this one was supposed to be. But this was a dry year for movies, and he didn't really want to do yard work on Darth Vader's birthday.

"Yeah, that sounds good. Anything you want, honey. Anything you want," Steve said while hiding his objection to seeing a made-for-TV movie. "Let me take a shower first, and we can get dressed and go to the noon showing."

"It's already 1:00," June replied, smiling in an obvious attempt to goad Steve into feeling a bit lazy. It worked.

"Holy shit, I didn't know it was that late!" Steve said and popped up. "I'm going to go jump into the shower!"

June smiled. "Don't jump in the shower; you could get hurt that way!"

Steve groaned as June had used his classic joke against him. "Oh, ha, ha," he said and pretended to bunny hop as he headed into the bathroom. They were only little jumps, as you can indeed get hurt if you jump in the shower.

Three hours later, Steve and his family were slowly walking out of the theater and to the car. "That was a truly terrible movie," June said with a sneering look.

Brian nodded and grunted and continued to scroll the endless scroll on his phone. "Yeah, it kinda sucked. But some of it was funny, I guess."

Kathy grunted back. "It's only funny if you're stupid."

Brian pretended to ignore Kathy but kicked her heel and made her hop. She slapped Brian on the back of the head.

"You dickhead!" Kathy popped. Brian smiled and took the slap that he knew he deserved. Generally, Brian and Kathy got along, and they both loved each other, yet there was always this underlying tit-for-tat that kept things amusing.

"Okay, knock it off and get in the car. Brian, can you put your phone down so you can get into the right car?" June said mockingly.

Brian slowly put down his phone with an exaggerated arm motion to sarcastically acknowledge his mother's command.

Kathy and June rolled their eyes in a coordinated display of mild contempt that only made Brian smile more.

I really do wonder if that is genetic, Steve thought as he sat behind the wheel and pushed the start button on the dash.

By this time, it was getting close to five, and it was indeed *Cinco de Drinko*—Marisol's was going to be uber-packed. Steve drove the short distance to the restaurant and found a decently close parking space. He was relieved that, for now, the parking lot wasn't completely filled, as he had seen it on other visits. Marisol's was indeed a really good Mexican restaurant, and everyone in the vicinity knew it.

June walked into the lobby and put Steve's name on the list.

"I gave them your phone number," June told Steve.

Steve picked his phone out of his pocket and kept it in his hand. "I'm on it, Your Highness!" He smirked and held his phone tightly so he would feel the buzz. The restaurant was already very crowded with large groups, and it was quite loud.

Steve and his family patiently waited for the rewarding buzz to be seated. Kathy, Brian, and June were all affixed to their phones. Steve surveyed the crowd and made note of a large assortment of boobs, all nicely dressed for the occasion. June had some fabulous boobs, but being a firmly based heterosexual male, Steve subconsciously eyed each cleavage and assessed. June had once asked what the big deal was about a woman's bust, and Steve assured her that it was genetic, and wasn't she lucky that he didn't ponder upon men's asses instead? June agreed but still whacked Steve on the head.

Steve jumped as his phone sprung to life with the text message that their table was ready.

"IT'S GO TIME," Steve announced while leaping up in an exaggerated military fashion, which scared the shit out of June.

"What the hell!" June popped up and hit Steve on his arm.

Steve smiled and pretended his arm was limp. "Well, if you didn't have your nose buried in your phone, you would have been prepared!"

June reflected and knew that Steve was right. "You're still a butt!"

Steve followed the tiny hostess to their table at the back of the restaurant by the bar. She was so skinny that Steve wondered how she could even walk or move. June and the kids followed, the latter staring down at their phones while sleepwalking to the table. Like ducklings, they blindly followed the family member in front of them.

As they sat down and the hostess glided away unexpectedly gracefully, Steve said, "I think she needs to eat more churros."

June chuckled and was deeply glad Steve liked fluffy women. Well, just one fluffy woman, which was her.

"You're terrible!" June chuckled again and opened the menu. She really didn't need to look as she always ordered the same chicken flautas with a side of sour cream. It had been her go-to for years. Also, there was something about the queso. It came in a cast iron skillet with a whole jalapeño pepper floating above the best cheese concoction known to man. June was lactose-intolerant and definitely jalapeño-intolerant, but that didn't stop her. There had been many a Sunday night spent in the bathroom when she didn't take her Lactaid and a pint of Pepto.

Steve looked over the menu briefly before putting it down. He knew what he wanted: a deep-fried chimichanga with guacamole. Like June, Steve had some food issues as well, but they were mostly centered around avocados. There was a tipping point between great guac and an hour on the toilet. Steve weighed the cost/benefit and typically sided with the guac.

Chips and the best salsa in the world showed up, along with water for all. The kids lazily picked at some chips, avoiding the salsa, still gazing at their hypnotizing screens. Steve and June chatted while they waited for the waitress. Or staff member. Or server. Or whatever the correct term was at that moment.

"What do you think you'll have?" June asked while piling a tablespoon of salsa on her chip. It was delicately balanced and held on to the chip by surface tension and a steady hand.

"I think I'll have the chimi with a side of acid reflux," Steve replied, proudly presenting his own guacamole-laden chip. Avocados gave Steve the worst case of indigestion, but he suffered through it for the delicious guacamole.

"You know you shouldn't eat the guac. It always makes you sick," June reminded him with a furrowed brow.

Steve loaded another chip and, while still chewing on the first one, said, "Well, what doesn't kill you makes you shit, and I'm okay with that today." As he plopped the chip in his mouth with a smile, he warned back, "Plus, you're going to queso yourself into a sleepless night if you're not careful."

June sighed and agreed. At least they would suffer together.

Veronica arrived to take their order. She was their personal server, it seemed. After seeing her so regularly over several years, she knew what they most likely wanted.

"Iced tea and a frozen margarita with salt for ya?" Veronica asked.

Steve nodded. "But of course. Only the best for us, you know. Today is an auspicious day." Steve really meant the Revenge of the Sith but allowed Veronica to stick with Cinco de Mayo.

"And what do you kids want?" Veronica asked rhetorically. She knew that they only wanted water but still thought to ask.

Kathy rolled her eyes almost imperceptibly at the thought of being called a kid, but to her credit, she held back. Kathy liked Veronica and had sort of grown up with her after all these years.

"I'll take water. Thank you," Kathy said.

"Water's cool," Brian added without looking up.

June was proud of Kathy for saying thank you. It was a small but meaningful gesture that many of her peers had never learned.

Veronica quickly came back with a tray full of drinks.

"One down and six to go!" Steve quipped and took a huge slurp out of the margarita.

Veronica laughed. While she had heard this joke, or a version of it, for years, it still made her chuckle. Steve was always a good spirit and, most importantly, a good tipper.

The queso showed up with another basket of chips. These were the fried flour tortilla chips, and they went perfectly with the queso.

"Oh my God, these are so good! I just love these chips!" June exclaimed. She said this every time she had them, and she wasn't lying. They were excellent chips—lightly fried triangles of delight.

Steve grunted in agreement and dug chip after chip into cheesy goodness. The kids also appreciated the chips and even the queso.

Just before the actual meal came, Steve and June were preliminarily stuffed.

"I need a tactical pause," Steve sighed.

June drank half her tea while Steve finished his margarita. It was important to finish each margarita in between Veronica's visits so she could ask if he wanted another. The answer was always yes up until the third one, whereupon June gave him that look.

Pausing after finishing the margarita in one slurp and suffering through a brain freeze, Steve looked around at the crowd. The restaurant had gotten a bit more crowded and louder, and several tables were downing actual pitchers of strawberry margaritas. By the tone of the tables, they were well into gallons.

Veronica arrived with a helper and a cart to put the trays on. The plates Marisol's used were classic thick ceramic and quite heavy. Most of the staff had pretty well-developed forearms, Veronica included.

"Here ya go," Veronica said as she put the last plate down. "Be careful—they are really, really hot," she added.

It was well known that the plates were delivered at the temperature of the surface of the sun. The chili sauce around the food was actually boiling. Still, they told each and every customer that the plates were hot, even though it was so apparently obvious to even the dumbest of people. That didn't include, however, drunk people. Veronica knew that this family knew, but still, she had to say it.

"Everything looks okay?" Veronica asked, knowing that it was.

"It looks perfect!" Steve replied and proceeded to nudge his white-hot plate around.

"Ouch, ouch, ouch!" he cried with each nudge. This was another of Steve's jokes that Veronica expected but, again, found a bit funny. Kathy and June asynchronously rolled their eyes. Brian didn't look up. Such was life on a Sunday at Marisol's.

Dinner was almost over, and Steve was on his third and final margarita. June and the kids had finished most of their meals after the gluttony of baskets of flour tortilla chips.

Steve noticed that the big tables were just getting served, and he marveled at the massive number of trays being transported at once. He wondered how they got the food all together at once.

Steve looked at June. "Do you think they just keep them all on a table with 10,000-degree lights on them while they get them all ready? I wonder if they get sunburned."

June considered this while taking a final swig of her tea. "I think they must. You know how hard it is to make everyone's plate at the same time and have it come out hot."

Steve was distracted from his ruminations when one of the drunker men at the larger table of ten people burned his hand on a molten plate.

"MOTHERFUCKER!" he said as he tossed his plate to the floor, splashing the diners at the big table next to his.

"She told you it was hot, you dumbass!" his wife/ girlfriend/ daughter/mistress said. She looked twelve and dressed like she was twenty-two, but they were obviously together.

"I didn't know it was that fucking hot, bitch!" he replied, molten refried beans coating his foot and leaking into his shoe.

Another drunk guy at the next table got a side of searing enchiladas on his leg. The plate had landed perilously close to his baby girl, who was in a carrier next to him, balanced on a chair.

"Watch it, you motherfucker, and watch your fucking mouth around these kids!" drunk guy number two said. While drunk guy number one looked like the classic East LA extra casting model, drunk guy number two was clearly a working-class father out with his extended family, complete with the abuela. He didn't see the irony that he was also using foul language in front of his own kids, but margaritas will do that to some people.

"Why don't you fucking make me, puto!" the LA villain said in one of the most comical comebacks ever voiced. Steve actually chuckled at that one, but he could feel his Spider-Man spidey sense kick in. This could go south quickly.

Both men, now standing, got closer. As they weighed each other up, the other men of the family started to push their chairs back.

"This shit's about to get real," Steve told June. "Get the kids out of here and go that way." Steve motioned towards the back of the restaurant, where there was an emergency exit.

June and Kathy immediately got up and whacked Brian out of his telephone stupor to follow them. Brian focused just long enough to see that both his parents were alarmed and instinctively moved with purpose. Only then did he notice the two tables in pre-war mode.

Marisol's manager and Veronica both came over to try to calm down the situation. Steve watched his family exit the back of the restaurant along with some other fairly observant families. The ones who remained all had their phones out in spectator mode.

Drunk men do what drunk men do and ignored Veronica and the other cries to stop—and so it began. Chairs were pushed over, sizzling food went flying, and random onlookers were burned with electric hot plates.

Steve held back but was a bit transfixed himself. He had never seen a full-on restaurant fight before. It was exciting but started to escalate with the introduction of the family man's children and grandparents.

Mr. East LA had gotten the upper hand for a moment, and he and his friends took turns pounding the father on the ground as he tried to crawl away. He crawled towards the other end of the table, where his grandmother was hiding behind a chair. His baby had been whisked away by someone else, but not his abuela.

Steve went dark, and without thinking, he moved to pull the woman out of the way of the flurry of punches and kicks. He got her to another table and sat her down, and Steve collapsed on the floor after a glancing blow managed to connect. His daze quickly wore off as he watched the fight continue. He looked around at the remaining customers, who were all filming for posterity and clicks.

The table next to Steve was filled with older teenagers who knew enough to hold the phone in landscape mode and pan around to get the whole scene—you know, to get the flavor of the action.

Steve noted that one of the teenagers was focusing his phone camera on him. Looking at the teens, and in his best Mexican accent, which was really terrible, he said, "Well, it wouldn't be Cinco de Drinko without some drunk Mexicans, eh, vato?" Steve's dad-humor had taken over to defuse the situation as he mugged for the camera, pleased with his joke.

The grandmother asked Steve if he was okay, as she saw he had been hit as he got her out of the way of the melee. "Thank you for saving me," she whispered, almost too low to hear. She was clearly in shock. "Are you okay?" she repeated.

Steve was momentarily taken aback by the kindness. "Yes, I'm okay, ma'am. I'm okay. Thank you," Steve said, and then gave her and the cameraman the classic OK sign. Steve looked through his circled thumb and index finger at the teenager, who then panned away just in time to see the police show up and end the fight. Being in a bit of shock himself, Steve got up and watched the cops take the East LA posse into custody. Paramedics arrived just as Steve was placing cash for the meal along with a larger-than-normal tip under his plate. He hoped Veronica was okay. He didn't see her before he left. It bothered him for the rest of the night.

Steve arrived at the car to meet June and the kids. June always drove home on Marisol nights due to Steve's three-margarita habit.

"I was so worried! What happened?" June sobbed as she rubbed Steve's head and examined him for injuries.

"Well, they drank, they fought, they made their ancestors proud," Steve joked. It was rare to be able to use a *Thor* quote.

June continued to look for wounds, but Steve reassured her that he was okay. "I even managed to do a good deed and get the abuela out of the way of the battle," Steve boasted.

"Well, you're a hero, then! Next time, let's try not to get involved," June said. She was proud of her husband but also didn't want to lose him to a bar fight. Or, in this case, a restaurant fight.

Kathy and Brian were half-listening as they searched to see if the fight had been posted yet. The constant refresh caused a flickering from the back seat as they drove home.

PART VII

Days passed, as they usually do in the ongoing march of routine. As May became June, Steve began his annual dad joke fest.

"What comes after May?" Steve asked.

June replied with an eye roll without looking up from her phone. Instagram was her favorite and only social media app. June liked to collect recipes. She was always surprised by what people created.

"Nothing. June usually comes first!" Steve blurted, raising his voice to emphasize FIRST. It was a private joke, as both Steve and June knew that Steve was always cognitive of those things in the bedroom.

"Hey, June!" Steve blurted again after the appropriate amount of time passed for the pinnacle of comedic timing.

June never moved. Scroll, scroll, scroll.

"If April showers bring May flowers, what does June bring?" Steve gushed.

Scroll, scroll, scroll.

"SANDWICHES!" Steve barked. Steve knew that he could always get a rise out of June with a sexist statement.

June looked up from her phone and performed an award-winning eye roll, complete with a perfectly synchronized head roll. It was a masterful work of art that their daughter had perfectly imitated and was pulled out only for the most egregious jokes.

"Don't you have something else to do? Anything? Mow the lawn? Please, God, mow the lawn. Something! Anything!" June lamented with an obvious inflection on *anything*. This was all accomplished with a dramatic repeat of the eye roll.

"You know I can do this all day," Steve said. And he was serious. He had well over a month's worth of jokes, and many just popped into his head, ready to pull out at the most appropriate moment. He was also secretly quoting *Captain America.*

June sighed. "I know you can," she said while shaking her head.

Steve was proud she knew the rest of the Captain's quote.

"Okay, fine. I've worn out my welcome here, I see. I'll go outside while it's still early and cool enough," Steve said. It could get upwards of 112 degrees in June, and Steve had worked into heat exhaustion on more than one occasion. Phoenix is the kind of hot where if your eyes are open, you can literally hear the *hissss* of moisture leaving your eye sockets.

June sighed again, shook her head, and went back to her phone. Secretly, she smiled because she liked the jokes and the attention but would never admit it. Secretly, Steve knew this, too.

Steve put on his working shoes of the moment, which were his yellow Crocs. He used the strap on the back of the shoes to make sure they stayed on. If you don't use the strap, you can easily walk out of them, and when using a sharp blade or weed eater, you're just tempting fate.

Steve was halfway through his edging when Kathy rushed outside, almost taking the screen door off its hinges.

"Holy shit, Dad, you've gone viral!" Kathy said while jumping over the water hose, almost tripping.

"What do you mean I've gone viral? I feel fine!" Steve joked, not knowing what the hell Kathy was talking about.

"There's a video of that fight at Marisol's, and you are in it. They're saying you're a racist fascist for being a white supremacist!" Kathy screamed, out of breath.

"That's stupid. I didn't even fight!" Steve blurted, clearly befuddled at how this could be.

"You said something about drunk Mexicans, and you held up a white power sign," Kathy said.

"What in God's name is a white power sign?" Steve asked. Steve was not clued into the shenanigans of the online 4Chan community, and as such, he had no clue as to what a supposed white power sign was.

"You know! White power! White supremacy? You've heard about this, right?" Kathy exclaimed as she held up the OK sign like a Nazi salute. The OK sign had been attributed to white supremacy by 4Chan message board users as a joke but had since become accepted as fact.

Steve pondered for a few moments and watched the video. It was pretty funny overall, but there was Steve talking about drunk Mexicans and holding up an OK sign to show everything was okay. Clearly, something had changed in that gesture, at least for the online crowd.

"Well, that's unfortunate. But I think I'll get over it," Steve mused.

"This isn't funny, Dad! People are all over it! My friends are all over it!" Kathy replied, raising her voice, doing a little stomp to emphasize *it*, and running back into the house as fast as she had run out. She slammed both doors to make a double point.

Steve continued to edge the expansive yard as the temperature crept to 105. Anything below 110 was okay, but it still wore on you.

He finished and put away the equipment before passing out, then shuffled about in his Crocs, hoping that Kathy would get over this and be okay. It wasn't pleasant when Kathy was moody, much less angry and moody. Steve went inside and walked upstairs to take a cold shower and a nap.

Steve affixed his CPAP machine, and it began hissing the soothing purr of cool air through the hose. He thought of the video again before chuckling to himself as he drifted off.

PART VIII

Steve awoke to June sitting next to him quietly and rubbing his back. Steve always liked waking up like this, and he also liked waking up to dinner, which was what he hoped had happened.

"Good morning. What day is it? Where am I, and who are you?" Steve mused to June as he pulled apart his CPAP mask, which was never pleasant.

"We have a small problem," June said, clearly worried. "Your video made it to Chatter, and they ID'd you. They have your actual name, and now they have our address!" June exclaimed, getting more worried.

"What in the holy hell is this bullshit?" Steve said.

"It's a thing these days. They also found out where you worked and tagged the City!" June cried. "The City only said, 'Thanks for the report; we'll look into it.'"

Steve sat up and grabbed his phone. "That's total bullshit! Let me see what they said!"

Suddenly, Steve realized he didn't even have Chatter. June didn't either.

"Well fuck, I've got to download the app. I don't even have a fucking account!" Steve said, as his thumbs worked feverishly, misspelling about every other word.

Steve downloaded and installed the app. He spent the next thirty minutes setting up an account with two-factor authentication and basic bullshit information to create a bare minimum shell account.

Steve pondered hard over his username. He didn't want anyone to be able to tie this account back to him.

"I need a name stupid enough to not attract attention but funny," Steve murmured to himself.

He thought for a bit, and after a few iterations and looking at his shoes at the bedside, he finally decided upon @yellowCrocs420. It was a stupid pot reference, and it was funny, so there it was. Steve felt quite pleased for a few moments until he realized that, oddly enough, the username was already taken.

"What the bloody hell?" Steve murmured.

So, @yellowCrocs421, it was. And after a few minutes, Steve started to search for the video.

It took a bit of doing, but he finally worked out how to navigate the application. It was somewhat intuitive, so in a matter of minutes, he was typing in "Steve Richardson."

Switching between Top and Latest on the search menu gave Steve enough bile to chew on. He put the phone down gently on the bed—this was to avoid throwing it.

By this time, June had left to go downstairs and prepare dinner. She could tell Steve needed to be alone and digest. She didn't know what the posts were saying, who said them, or why. She knew the results, and June was the kind of person where she could nicely shelve thoughts if she needed to.

Kathy came downstairs, wiping the makeup from her teenager's tear-stained eyes.

"Mom, this is horrible! I don't know what to do!" Kathy cried. In fact, she started to sob again in the kitchen.

June hugged her and made her sit down at the kitchen table. It was cool to the touch and about as informal as you could get. That comfort of familiarity helped calm Kathy to a sniffled cry as June rocked her back and forth like a baby.

"We'll work it out. It will all be okay," June said, doing her best to hide her own anxiety.

Steve walked downstairs and sat in his overstuffed chair in the family room. Like the kitchen table, it embodied calmness. Well, it tried. Today was a tough one.

Steve turned on the television and, in his numbness, found *The Lord of the Rings: Return of the King*. It was the ultimate comfort movie series that Steve and June watched over holiday weekends, and they often fell asleep at the third hour of the extended version. It typically required five nights to finish.

June finished up a breakfast dinner that she had been working on. Kathy set the table silently. It was quiet except for the murmurings of an ever-complaining Frodo Baggins. Steve thought that if Frodo would just put the One Ring on a rope and drag it around, Sauron might forget he had it. The One Ring would just live its life dragging through the dirt and then INTO THE FIRES OF MOUNT DOOM! That might make it a shorter movie, though.

Steve smelled the beef bacon and toast and turned off the television. He wandered into the kitchen silently and sat at the table. Breakfast dinner was also a comfort dinner, and Steve knew June made it for a reason. Sometimes there was no reason, but today there was.

They pulled Brian away from his Xbox, and he begrudgingly flopped into a chair. His eyes brightened a bit as he saw the eggs and pancakes that June had made. He didn't appear upset in any way. He just had a bit of dull eye glaze from hours of playing another shooting game.

Steve had Brian pull his gaming headphones off the top of his head, where he kept them while not actually engaged in a world-ending battle. It was like a hat that he never noticed was there.

"Whatcha been up to?" Steve asked Brian as he served his plate. Steve hoped that he wouldn't take an extra pancake.

"Just playin'," Brian deadpanned.

"Well, it's good to change things up a bit. You don't want to get stale," Steve said sarcastically.

Kathy rolled her eyes on Brian's behalf. Brian just did a *humph* and shrugged his shoulders. June kept eating and never looked up.

Steve ate for a bit, and after he finished his pancakes, he took the remainder of the milk.

"Have you heard anything else?" Steve casually asked Kathy.

Kathy stirred her food and sat quietly for a moment. "Yeah, it's pretty bad, actually. Thanks for asking," Kathy replied sulkily.

"Like what?" he asked.

"I don't want to talk about it. It's just bad," Kathy shrank some more.

Steve and June knew that when Kathy didn't want to talk about something, she wouldn't, at least at the time. She typically saved it up for an emoting session around the same time of the month. It was as regular as clockwork.

Kathy pretended to eat for a few more minutes. It was just enough to give the appearance of eating without anything actually making it into the mouth. June knew she wasn't eating, as she had practiced the art at business lunch meetings. But at this point, you needed to fight your battles appropriately. This wasn't one of them.

June picked up the dishes as Kathy passive-aggressively stomped out of the room and up the stairs. Brian literally scraped the plate clean, put on his headset, got a Code Red out of the fridge, and slinked upstairs. He always kind of looked like he was walking through water.

June and Steve sat down in the family room and resumed the movie. It was 8:30 pm, so they had about an hour before heading to bed. They sat quietly and watched Frodo take (not drag) the One Ring into Mordor after escaping Shelob. After a bit, June reached over, took Steve's hand and held it.

"It will be okay. Tomorrow is a new day, and we'll deal with it, whatever *it* is," June whispered lovingly. Steve really appreciated that, and it was one of his last good memories for a long time.

Steve was dreading Monday. His name was out there. His address. His employer. And most importantly, a score of bored Karens all bent on finding their next Target of Outrage™. Deep down, Steve prepared himself for the worst, given that it was worse to use the wrong pronouns at work than to steal a computer.

Steve and June walked upstairs and turned on some rain sounds. He affixed the CPAP and lay motionless for two hours as sleep eventually crept in.

PART IX

Steve woke up at around 4 a.m. It was roughly three hours before his typical waking, and after thirty minutes of wishing to return to sleep, he just ripped off the CPAP and sat at the edge of the bed…for another thirty minutes.

The Chatter feed continued to spew all kinds of nonsense. User @autohack423 claimed that Steve was a member of Stormfront. User @Progfrog31 agreed and vomited forth that Steve's children were blond Hitlerjugend. Deflated, Steve made his way to the bathroom. His hands began to shake as he hunched on the toilet to scroll in solitude.

"Fuck, I hope Kathy doesn't see these," Steve muttered as he poured over the growing list of insane comments. Many were memes that tried to personify Steve in an exercise of mind-reading projection. It was then that Steve saw his employer was tagged.

"Hey @COPHX, did you know that your employee is a white supremacist?" wrote Frankie, known by his original username @FrankieGTHollywood. Steve read and reread the comments from Frankie, who had ridiculous neon hair that looked like a caricature of a gay cholo from the hood.

"What are the chances that they will even see this? The internet is huge," Steve murmured.

Steve knew he would have to face the outside world soon enough, so he decided to get dressed, skip breakfast, and slip out of the house before anyone else was awake. He left the radio off as he drove to work through the long stretches of warehouses and tire shops. In silence, Steve's mind shifted from what might happen to what did happen to what probably wouldn't happen. A forty-minute drive seemed to take three days. Steve finally made it into his favorite parking space, where he sat in his car for another fifteen minutes before taking the long walk into City Hall.

Before he slunk into his cube, Steve went to the cafeteria to get a breakfast burrito. The café's breakfast burritos were practically the only edible meal they made. Inside the prison-style eatery, there were at least eight cameras, as if the employees were criminals.

Who is going to steal from here? And what? The packages of barrio candy? Steve thought. He then thought that sounded racist— maybe he was a white supremacist after all.

Steve watched as his bacon burrito with onions and jalapeños was built. The old Mexican woman behind the sneeze shield was a true maestro in this realm. Sadly, that did not translate to the famed chicken nugget sandwich and cold green beans that would be served later.

As he took his burrito, Steve asked for two extra salsas, which amounted to two ounces of really tasty salsa for $.50. Everything had a price, including the plastic forks that would break upon the second bite.

Steve slowly walked into the elevator and then onto his floor. The walk through the office was grueling, and while it seemed like nobody was there, as they were working below their cube walls, all attention was fixed upon Steve in his walk of shame.

He sat down, booted his computer, and logged in. Now was time for serious work, which meant unwrapping the burrito.

After a few bites, the mousy girl who served as the HR manager's aide came by. Steve didn't even know her name, as she usually stayed in her cube with pictures of her cats. Yes, she was that type of female.

"Hey, Steve, do you have a moment to talk to Briana?" the mousy girl who likes cats asked.

She smiled lightly as Steve said, "Okay," rewrapped his burrito, and stood up slowly. Steve followed her. He knew what this was about.

Mousy girl took Steve past the HR manager's office into the small conference room, which had the blinds closed. Inside sat Briana, Steve's boss Kurt, Rose, the director, and two policemen.

Steve's stomach literally yelped in surprise at the sight of the law and tried to leave his body through his anus. Whatever he had imagined, this was much worse than Steve's worst-case scenario.

Briana spoke first. "Steve, are you aware of a video you are in that's spreading on social media?" she asked.

"A little. My daughter saw it," Steve answered hesitantly. It was as if Steve's soul was leaking out of his shoes below the long conference table.

"Then I'm sure you're aware of the reactions and the volatility of the situation?" Briana inquired.

Steve looked down for a moment before answering. "A little. It is completely out of context. Nothing happened like they are talking about."

"What do you say happened, Steve?" Briana asked, smirking slightly like the jackal she was.

"There was a fight. I helped protect an old lady. That was it. All the other bullshit is made up out of whole cloth!" Steve implored with visible sweat on his brow. He didn't mean to raise his voice, but he could tell that the end justified the means.

"I'm sorry, Steve, but we're terminating your employment effective immediately pending a civil servant review process. The perception is that you presented some problematic racial actions. We don't take this lightly, and we hope you understand that our first responsibility is to maintain the organization's stability," Briana said, looking to both sides of her for nods of agreement from the mute Kurt and Rose. The policemen just stared at Steve.

While Kurt wouldn't look at Steve, Rose finally found the words to sum up the situation. "We wish you the best in your future endeavors, Steve," Rose said without a hint of empathy as she stood up from the table. That was the sign to leave. Steve had always hated Rose. She was a ruthless leader, had favorites, and made knee-jerk decisions that would rapidly be changed or reversed. And now she was rid of Steve.

"Are we done here?" Steve asked. He also thought that he was, in fact, done.

"We are," Briana said curtly.

Steve stood up methodically and began walking towards the closed door. "I'll go pack my things," Steve said.

As he stood up, the policemen moved in. They didn't get close to Steve but made it clear he was within taser range.

"You don't need to. We will safely pack your things and send them to you," Briana said. "I'll also need your badge."

Steve separated his badge from its necklace-carrying case and dropped it onto the table, making a satisfactory smacking sound as it hit. He then turned around sharply and silently walked into the hallway. Kurt never said a word.

As Steve did another long walk of shame to the elevator, the prairie dog heads of his coworkers peeped above their cube walls. Rick was not shy.

"Dude, this is so not fair. This is bullshit!" Rick shouted.

The policemen turned and glared at Rick as they walked by.

"Please sit down, sir, SIR!" one cop yelled as a threat was evaluated. The last thing they wanted was a rabble-rouser. Rick was undeterred.

"You guys think he needs a police escort? Such bullshit!" Rick blurted as he slowly began to sit down, mumbling as he did.

As he neared the elevators, Steve looked back to see a small crowd at the front desk. Among the group was Michelle, who looked Steve in the eye, shook her head, and turned around.

PART X

Steve woke up on his own. The previous twenty-four hours were a blur, and the dreams had been a true horror show. As his eyes cleared, he rolled over to check the time on his phone. It was 11:32 am, and Steve had been asleep for thirteen hours.

June walked in and sat down on the edge of the bed next to Steve's legs and began rubbing and patting his stomach with a "there-there" pat.

"How do you feel?" June asked, maintaining a slight tone of neutrality in her voice. Steve recognized this type of cadence and knew that June wasn't happy. Not mad, but just not happy.

"I'm doing okay," Steve lied. His stomach turned into a knot again, and he felt the *gurgle, gurgle, rumble bubble pop* out of his bowels. "I've got to head to the bathroom."

June stood up and walked away. "Feel better," she said as she left.

Steve walked slowly to the bathroom and sat on the throne. He made sure to flip on the vent to spare the house from the horrors about to be expelled from his lower intestine.

Scrolling through and reliving the digital doom that had thrust itself upon him, his face became hot. Some of the rants had become personal and had spread to mention June. @FrankieGTHollywood had been industrious and looked up

Steve's name to find his house, and then he found June's name as the co-buyer.

"Hey @stjoeAZ, do you know your employee June is married to a white supremacist?" @FrankieGTHollywood posted.

The myriads of replies performed great feats of mindreading on what June and Steve believed, and more than a few replies tagged June's hospital.

Feeling defeated, Steve let the phone slip from his hands to land with a thud on the floor, where, as far as he was concerned, it could stay. With his head bowed, he sat in silence until his legs got too numb to stand.

June was making a late breakfast when Steve eventually made his way into the kitchen. He poured a glass of orange juice and slid into a chair. Steve loved orange juice, but today, it tasted like orange juice and toothpaste. The thrill was gone.

June methodically tossed the eggs around while the bread was toasting. Steve truly liked her breakfasts, and it was a sign that all was well in the world. But today, things were not well.

Steve remained quiet while June cooked and watched through the kitchen window as the birds outside ate. June was responsible for pounds and pounds of bird seed each week to feed the birds. Thousands of birds seemingly depended upon her for their sustenance. Just seeing them eat what June had provided reminded him of her cooking their dinner. June cared for living creatures of all kinds, including Steve.

June plated up the food, gathered forks and napkins, and sat down at the table. She poured herself some juice and drank half before talking.

"So, you took a while," June said.

"I had to work out some things," Steve said with a smirk. He started to eat while wondering if he should tell June what he had seen online. After watching June eat with little care in the world, he decided not to. Again, he would play the odds that nothing else would happen, and this would all die down.

Steve and June chatted a bit about the day, what Steve's employment plans were, and how they would get by on her income for a while. Steve relaxed a bit when he realized June wasn't mad, just concerned.

"I still don't understand how all this happened," June said as she finished her last bite.

"The internet is a crazy place. People are crazy. Apparently, some have nothing better to do than to scour social media for their cause," Steve mused. "I just hope it quiets down so I can start to interview."

"I'm glad to see that this hasn't got to you," June said as she patted his leg.

Steve let the facts of the matter go unsaid. June didn't have a Chatter account and was blissfully unaware. The kids had moved on since the first day, as kids do. They went on to the next dance craze, game, or the social contagion of the week.

Steve cleaned the dishes and threw away the napkins. It was the least he could do.

He poured a glass of water and sat down in the living room to watch television, settling on a mindless episode of *Hogan's Heroes* and passively gazing at the screen. Familiar television was calming and still allowed him to think. He drifted into the show as his mind calmed.

The telephone rang. They still had a landline, but it was rare that they used that phone. Steve kept it up for a backup.

June answered the phone with an inquisitive voice.

Steve heard mumbles and affirmations, which rose into a crescendo of angry words. Steve's gut punched him again.

June walked into the living room, sat down on the sofa, and grabbed a pillow.

"I've been fired. It's done," June said, tears starting to well. June rarely cried, but when she did, it was so sad to watch. Like everything else, she did it with zeal.

Steve sat in the recliner with a blank gaze, unable to move or speak. How had this all happened so quickly and with such finality? This was a waking nightmare, and it wasn't letting up.

"I'm so sorry," Steve murmured, still staring blankly at the television.

June's tears started to slowly drip down her cheeks. "I truly don't understand this. I've worked there for ten years, and they didn't even want to talk to me."

June stood up after a time and walked into the bedroom. Steve continued to sit and watch the antics of Hogan into the night. When he finally went to bed, June was asleep. He rolled carefully beside her, adjusting his CPAP, and placed his arm on her hip. June sighed a bit in her sleep as Steve lay there motionless and awake until three.

PART XI

When Steve awoke after what was one of the worst weeks of his life, June wasn't there. He lay there for another hour until his bladder got him out of bed. He walked into the bathroom and did his "morning doody," as Steve liked to say.

June was sitting in the kitchen, looking at her phone. As she scrolled, Steve wandered in, poured some juice, and sat down.

"Watcha doin?" Steve said before drinking half the glass. The juice actually tasted good today.

"Well, half our friends on OpenBook have dropped me. The other half say how sorry they are I'm married to you," June said. She never looked up.

Steve sat quietly. "You never liked them anyway, I'm sure."

"How do you know who I like? At least I had some semblance of friends, and now they're gone. And the rest hate you," June exclaimed, raising her voice above her normally serene tone.

Steve continued to sit and slowly drink his juice. "You know none of this is real. It didn't happen like they say it did. You were there!" Steve hit back.

June continued to scroll. "You know it doesn't matter what reality is. The online gang defines what happened, and then others repeat it, and on it goes. It's called viral for a reason!"

Understanding that June was exactly right and that he was indeed fucked and had spread the woe to his wife, Steve went back into the bedroom to lie down. June kept scrolling.

CHAPTER TWO

"Thank you for your post @FrankieGTHollywood. We take things like this seriously and we'll look into it right away."

Contact PHX (@COPHX)

PART I

Steve sat in his easy chair, scrolling through endless channels on the TV, waiting for something—anything—to pique his interest. It had been two months since the Event That Shall Not Be Named, AKA The Day. It was a few minutes after noon when Steve had woken up to begin his day, if it could even be called a day. The time that used to be filled with work was now full of television, vodka, and food. Steve had gained well over twenty pounds in his despair. It seemed like more, as he now took heavy breaths like a fat man would.

June walked into the living room and watched Steve for a brief moment before entering the kitchen. After being fired from her hospital job, June had landed a pretty decent position as a hospice nurse. This allowed her to set her schedule and made her a bit more valuable—valuable enough not to be fired from some online bullshit that she had nothing to do with.

As she walked by, she noted his ever-present steel mug. It was the type of flagon you could get at a fan festival formerly and have unlimited soda for the $35 price of the cup. Now, instead of soda, Steve filled it with cheap vodka and the mixer of the day. Today, it was lemonade. Some days, it was just vodka.

"June, do you think you could make me a sammich?" Steve asked, thinking he was somewhat humorous with that reference. June did not agree.

"Don't you think you should get up and maybe move around a bit? You know, do something unusual?" June quipped while selecting the ingredients to make a bologna sandwich.

June was still optimistic that Steve would pull out of this depression and start looking for work again. He had tried applying to a few other municipalities and even the county, but with those kinds of jobs, it took a long time to even get an interview. In the meantime, Steve used this as an excuse to sleep, drink, and eat his way through the process until getting that call. June longed for some purpose for Steve, even a hobby.

Steve said sarcastically, "But I am doing something unusual. I'm not watching the news." All Steve did was watch the news and scroll.

Steve continued to scroll and scroll. But nothing interested him in the least, and as noon crept into one o'clock, there was a new set of shows to pick from.

"Well, that's a start, I suppose," June replied as she brought Steve his sandwich and a can of soda. She sat on the sofa and watched Steve from the corner of her eye as she pretended to scroll on her phone. "Do you think you've been drinking too much?" June asked, still pretending to scroll.

Steve let out an audible sigh and took a bite of his sandwich. "I have yet to start," Steve quipped, which clearly irritated June.

"That's what I'm afraid of, Steve," June replied. "It's really starting to affect the family. Even Brian has started to notice, and that's saying something. Kathy isn't around much if you haven't noticed, and you are the reason!"

"That's on her," Steve mumbled.

June put down her phone.

"No, Steve. That's on you," she said, punctuating his name with a hard S.

Steve stared blankly at the show he had finally picked. It was an episode in a series about some Amish man who made backyard moonshine.

June waited a few minutes for Steve to respond, but he didn't, so she got up and started to walk away. "When you figure this out and find the old Steve again, let me know. I don't like this new Steve much. He's a bit of an asshole."

Steve watched as the people on TV decided what flavor the English would like most for today's moonshine batch. He ate the rest of his sandwich and went into the kitchen to mix another drink. Or not. Straight out of the bottle seemed preferable.

PART II

Later that night, Steve emerged from the bathroom and headed to the dinner table. It was just after six, and he had been doom-scrolling on the toilet for over an hour. His legs were just barely working again from the numbness as he sat back down.

Steve sat slumped in his chair and continued to scroll. June was absent-mindedly going through the motions of making dinner, although she tried to hide her anxiety. After this afternoon's conversation, she really wanted to present her best in hopes of lighting up the dark mood that had come over the house.

"I'm making some oven burritos, so I hope you're hungry!" June chimed. She pulled the burritos out of the oven and set them down to cool. They were hefty burritos made from fresh tortillas. June was pretty sure that the Hispanic women who made them had been doing that for generations.

Steve never looked up and said, "Are they the ground beef kind or the chorizo kind?"

"They're the chorizo kind. I know you like those best. They have onions and rice and a bit of refried black beans," June replied, getting out the cutlery to set the table.

Steve sat motionless as he scrolled. "Do we have any guac?" he asked.

June finished setting the table. "We had some avocados that were going bad, so I salvaged a few and cut out the black stuff," she said.

She moved over to the fridge to get drinks for everyone, hoping Steve would be okay with just water.

As she finished, Steve got up and went to get his flagon. He poured some margarita mix into the cup and filled the rest with vodka. A few ice cubes finished the drink. Steve was well aware he was supposed to use tequila in margaritas, but ever since the Incident-That-Shall-Not-Be-Discussed, he couldn't tolerate tequila.

June watched in growing despair as Steve took a big gulp and plopped back into his chair. He actually plopped as if his legs had given out at the last minute and collapsed into a controlled fall.

"Supper!" June shouted at the bottom of the stairs. If that didn't work, she was prepared to text them to come down. And if that didn't work, she would disconnect the Wi-Fi.

After a few minutes, she heard the *plop plop* of Brian's oversized shoes coming down the stairs. Following was the *tap tap* of Kathy. They were both still engrossed in their phones.

"Why don't y'all look up from your magnetic devices to walk down the stairs? It's only a matter of time before you fall. I've seen those accidents. It ain't pretty," June implored.

"Oh, Mom, don't be a pooper!" Kathy replied, never once looking up.

"Don't pooper me! Once, we had a patient who fell down the stairs, and his leg got turned around backward. We had to turn it around or cut it off. One of the two." June was half serious. "The patient broke his leg in two places. Metal plates fixed that."

Kathy huffed in protest. "That's gross, Mom. I get it."

Brian finally looked up and put his phone down on the table. "So, did they cut it off?" he asked as he sat down next to his dad.

June thought quickly. "It doesn't matter. He lived. And he started watching his feet when he was going down the stairs; you can be sure of that."

Brian snickered and took a drink from his glass as he eyed Steve's mug. "Having a dinner drink? You think I could do that? You know, sharing is caring," Brian said as he smiled and put down his glass with a clink.

"What's it to ya? Mind your own business," Steve blurted before swigging another mouthful of his monstrous vodka nastiness.

June stopped plating the burritos and looked at Steve, who hadn't looked up once since he sat down. Her demeanor seemed to change the room's temperature, making it feel like it had dropped ten degrees. Kathy looked at her dad, and then at her mom, then continued to scroll on her phone.

Brian sat for a second, looking confused. "You're a grumpy Gus, Dad," he said, then immediately re-engaged himself in his digital world.

Steve slowly looked up to face Brian. "Why don't you keep your fucking comments to yourself for a change? Huh?" Steve's face was notably red, and he was sweating a bit.

Silence filled the room as Kathy and Brian looked at their dad as one would look at a talking cat.

Steve slowly lowered his head and continued to scroll. He took another large gulp, his thumb continuously flicking.

"Steve. Please, Steve," June besought.

Steve looked up and glared at June. "What? I'm tired of being demeaned by my own children!" he said, his voice raising at the end.

June set the plates of burritos around the table and went back to get the bowl of guacamole and the chips. She returned and sat down at the other side of what had become a drunk, then turned to face him.

"You're on the border of abusive, Steve. Put the drink down, and let's all enjoy this dinner that I spent the better part of the afternoon making. For you!" June said.

"Don't tell me what to or what not to do. I'm sick of it. I'm trying my best, and all anyone can do is rag on me. Don't forget, I'm the victim in this family. I'm still the victim to this day!" He glared at everyone at the table and took another drink.

"We have all suffered through this. Remember, I lost my job too. Kathy has been the target of so much hatred that it's impacted her grades. Not that you noticed," June replied, never taking her eyes off Steve.

Steve lowered his mug and stared at June. "What's there to notice? Her grades weren't that great anyway."

Kathy looked up and away from her phone. She looked at June to see just how offended she should be. June's expression said a lot.

"I think you've had enough to drink today, Steve!" June said, raising her voice at the end with an emphasis on "Steve!"

Steve took a last swig and slammed his cup on the table. The metal clang caused everyone to jump. "Fine! I think I'll have another!" Steve yelled, now obviously drunk.

He walked over to the fridge, but June beat him to it. Since Steve couldn't walk straight, he was naturally slow.

June opened the freezer, snatched the vodka bottle, and ran to the sink.

Steve staggered toward her in a half-hearted chase, but June had opened the bottle and was defiantly decanting it into the garbage disposal. Steve tried to wrench it from her grip and partially succeeded in doing so. He hip-checked her to get her away from the sink. But June's resolve won the day, and he watched the last drops being emptied into the drain.

He slumped on the sink, both hands holding him up, staring longingly at the empty bottle. "Goddammit, June!" he roared. His recently acquired red drinker's face had turned an even deeper shade of red.

June walked away, sat back down at the dinner table, and began to pick at her food. It was cold now, but June was in a bit of shock and sat just staring ahead.

Kathy bolted and ran upstairs, yelling, "I fucking hate this! I HATE IT!"

Brian slowly stood up. He looked at his mother, and then his father, and back again at his mother. Then he put his phone in his pocket and walked slowly upstairs with his eyes downcast.

Steve moved away from the sink and stumbled into the living room to watch TV. He managed to catch himself at least three times before collapsing into his recliner. He put up his feet and turned on a movie. It didn't matter what the movie was, as he immediately fell asleep, mouth agape.

June continued to eat a few more bites and then cleaned the table. She was going to do what she usually did and package the leftovers for lunches. She stopped and looked at the plates of food.

"Fuck this," June said and tossed the food into the trash.

PART III

Nighttime became morning, and Steve continued to sleep in the recliner. June had gone to bed early the previous night but had a sleepless night thinking about what she had to do.

She showered, got dressed, and applied makeup in an automaton manner. She went through the motions, finished up, walked slowly downstairs, and sat next to Steve. She was nervous and angry all at the same time as she waited for him to come to from his drunkenness.

"Steve," June said. She repeated his name more than ten times before he stirred.

Steve slowly opened his eyes and tried to focus. He was somewhat startled at how late in the morning it was, not really remembering how he had gotten into the chair.

"Whoa. What time is it? Is it past noon?" Steve slurred, still a bit drunk all those hours later.

"Steve, we need to talk," June said.

Steve knew that whatever had happened, June wasn't happy, and that made him unhappy. He looked at June with dim eyes and started to open his mouth to reply. She didn't give him a chance.

"Last night at dinner, you were more than a drunk ass. You were a violent drunk ass," June said, her eyes not blinking or turning away. Steve began to get worried.

"What did I do? What could I have possibly done?" Steve protested, trying hard to remember the night before. He had flashes of thoughts and began to dread what he remembered, even if it wasn't clear.

"You yelled at the children. Demeaned them. You attacked me when I took your booze. That and the cursing and tantrums…it's too much, Steve," June said. "And you need to leave."

Steve blinked a few times to understand. "What do you mean I need to leave?" He began to quiver as he realized he had crossed a line.

"You need to live somewhere else, at least for the time being. I don't care where you go. You've attacked your family and tried to hurt me. You can go anywhere, but you just can't stay here," June explained.

Steve's face went from slightly red to apple red as he started to cry. "June, I can make this right! I can stop drinking! I can look for a job!"

"Please stop, Steve! I'm not talking about divorce. For the sake of you and your family, you need to spend some time getting yourself together. You're a mess, and you're taking it out on us!" June said, holding back her own tears. "You need to leave when you're sobered up. If you come back before you're better, I'll file a restraining order."

"What is better?" Steve asked while drying his eyes.

"Stop your drinking, actually look for work, get a hobby… something!"

"I'm sorry," he said as he got up to go pack a bag. "I'm so very sorry."

"I know. And I forgive you," she said to him as he left the room. "But we just can't live like this any longer. I'm sorry too," she added.

"I'll say goodbye to the kids, and then I'll leave," Steve said, turning once more.

June winced as she watched Steve turn to go up the stairs. "Don't worry. I'll let them know. They are already at school. And you can call anytime, as long as you're sober!"

Steve packed his largest suitcase with everything he thought he would need for a month. He figured he could pull it together by then.

"Let's see. Underwear, ten shirts, a few socks," Steve rattled on as he packed. He then went into the bathroom to pack some razors, his toothbrush, and deodorant. As he packed his toothbrush, he began to sob.

June sat downstairs crying silently as she listened to Steve crying. She was really regretting her decision, but she couldn't allow the status quo to continue. It was destroying their lives, and she needed to limit the damage. As harsh as that sounded to June, it was reality.

Steve collected himself and brought his suitcase downstairs. He almost forgot his phone charger but picked it up and put it in his pocket.

"I'll put money into our Merchant Bank Visa card to free up some credit every month. Give me a call to let me know you're okay," June said.

Steve nodded and kissed her on the cheek. "I will be okay. I'll get myself sorted out."

June watched as Steve turned to leave. He grabbed his keys from the little table by the front door.

"I love you, Steve," June said, tears welling up in her eyes.

"I love you too, honey," Steve replied, then opened the door and walked out into his new hell.

PART IV

Steve loaded the car and sat. His suitcase barely fit into his Kia Soul, but what the car lacked in size, it made up in gas mileage. When Steve used to work, it was the perfect commuter car. Now, it was a small casket.

"What am I doing?" Steve asked himself out loud. He put his head on the steering wheel as June watched him from the upstairs window.

Steve pulled out his phone and opened his contacts. As he flicked through the alphabet, he found that he had few friends; most of the numbers were for work contacts, which were now pointless as Steve had assumed the role of pariah.

Steve made it to the *Rs* and saw Rick's phone number. He thought for a moment, then sent a text.

"Dude, I have a problem," Steve texted. He waited patiently for a few minutes and saw the bouncing dots of Rick's pending reply.

"You sure do, you dumb shit!" Rick replied. "Just kidding, dude, lol. What's up?"

Steve thought about what to say next. He had never been much for maintaining the digital communication expected in social relationships these days, which was obvious due to his lack of non-work friends.

"Dude, I need a place to stay for a bit to get things sorted out at home. Can I crash?" Steve asked, his thumbs struggling with each letter.

The dots came back faster this time. "Sure, dude! I'll shoot you my address! Come on over, bud!" Rick replied. He seemed authentically happy at the idea of having Steve stay with him. But then again, Rick was unpredictable at baseline.

Steve pasted Rick's address into the GPS and set off. June watched him drive away, then moved away from the window and onto the bed to cry.

Steve stopped by the store to gather a few things to bring over to Rick's, most of which happened to be vodka and margarita mix. As he checked out, the clerk looked at all the booze and the assortment of chips, nuts, and cheese crackers.

"So… you're going for the bachelor diet?" the clerk joked.

Steve looked at the clerk with dead eyes. "Yeah. Something like that. Thanks!"

The clerk finished scanning the haul and glanced over at the cash register. "That will be \$321.54, sir," he said demurely.

Steve took out his debit card and went through the payment process. The payment was declined. He tried another. Declined.

"God dammit!" Steve shouted. The clerk jumped. Steve noticed and calmed himself down as much as he could, then remembered which card June had allowed him to keep and presented it to the clerk. The approval finally came, and Steve slowly rolled the cart out of the store and loaded his car.

Steve backed violently out of his space and raced through the parking lot. He was still fuming and mumbling to himself about the declined cards. It had really burned him.

He pulled up to Rick's apartment complex. It was in one of the rougher low-income areas in Phoenix, which meant a mixture of homeless, welfare homes, and hard-working blue-collar families. There were more than a few undocumented families around, often living together to help pay the rent. They were quiet enough but were often taken advantage of by the area's rougher criminal element, which was prevalent.

Laden with his purchases, Steve made his way through the maze of stairs and hallways and regretted getting so much all at once from the store. Using his head, as his arms were full of liquor, Steve bashed a few times on the door.

He heard some rustling, and Rick finally showed up to open the door. By then, Steve's arms were shaking under the weight of the bags.

"Dude!" Rick shouted as he opened the door and took some of the bags away from Steve. "Get your ass into mi casa, you troublemaker!" The aroma of weed and sweat wafted out. Steve twitched his nostrils.

He shuffled into the small and messy apartment, then stopped to look around at what he had gotten himself into. There was an old pizza box on the kitchen bar, which was exactly what Steve had expected. Empty cans of energy drinks and some off-brand hard seltzer were literally on every flat surface. The sink was full of what appeared to be a week's worth of old, crusted food. Steve's expectations of how Rick's house was pretty on point. He sighed and brought the bags into the kitchen, where he looked for a clear spot.

"Dude, just put them down anywhere. I'll clean this place up for ya. I just didn't have a lot of warning," Rick said.

Steve massaged his cramping arms and sat down in one of the few dining chairs Rick had around a breakfast bar.

"I really appreciate you doing this for me," Steve said. "Really, I do. I'm in a bad spot."

"Dude, what happened? Ever since the cops took you away, it's been a constant politically correct shit show at work. Shit, I've had to go through about five classes on everything from racism to how not to talk to women! It's so fucking stupid!" Rick complained as he rifled through the bags to see what Steve had brought. He smiled at the bottles of vodka.

Steve sighed as he piled a few empty cans away from him so he could put his arm on the table. "June kicked me out. I was an ass and took my anger out on the kids and her. I've been drinking a lot."

"Yeah, I can see that, bud!" Rick laughed as he hoisted two large jugs of cheap vodka out of the bags.

Steve sighed. "I need to cut back, but this thing has wrecked me, Rick."

"Dude, what happened was bullshit. The people who did this to you need to pay. Those fuckers at work need to pay. It's all piss-ant PC shit!" Rick snorted, then started to make space on the kitchen bar for the alcohol.

"Yeah, it sucked. That's for sure," Steve agreed.

Rick started to unpack the rest of the bags and put the groceries in their places. Surprisingly, his cupboard was remarkably organized—A far cry from the rest of his house.

"Dude, you didn't deserve anything that you got. What about June and the kids? I know she kicked you out, but are they good?" Rick asked.

"June got fired because of me. The kids got harassed because of me. Our neighbors ignore us because of me," Steve said, his voice trailing off.

"No! That's bullshit, dude! It was because of those shits that posted it and kept plugging away to get you cancelled. They think they're all high and mighty, but one day, someone's going to kick their ass for what they do to people! You can't just destroy someone's life and expect to keep yours!" Rick railed, slamming the cupboard door.

Steve thought about Rick's words for a moment. "Well, maybe, but in my case, I deserved it."

Rick walked over to sit down by Steve. "Dude, that's bullshit. Don't take it! You did nothing wrong! Don't think about things like that. Hey, listen, you hang at my place for as long as you need. I got sheets for the sofa, but we will need to buy a pillow. I got a few sofa pillows there, but that's about it. I even have a cleanish blanket."

Steve looked up at Rick. "Thanks, dude. Thank you!"

"Mi casa es su casa!" Rick said. "I will text you the Wi-Fi password. Maybe you can remember it. It's bubblebutt69."

Steve chuckled. Of course, it was.

"What's the network name?" Steve asked, expecting something profane. He wasn't disappointed.

"It's suckmydick69, all one word," Rick laughed. "Nobody knows it's me, so who the fuck cares?"

Steve was pretty sure that anyone who knew Rick knew that the suckmydick69 network was his. "I never would have guessed," he said.

Steve and Rick cooked some frozen pizzas and poured glasses of vodka. Steve had his special vodka margarita while Rick just added some Coke. As night fell, they ate their bachelor dinners watching TV. Rick had, oddly enough, a really nice, mounted TV. It was 70 inches, and he had done a good job of hiding the wires. Rick sat in a recliner while Steve lay with his head on the arm of a reasonably comfortable sofa. They finished watching *Moonshiners* on the History Channel, and Rick knocked back the rest of his drink.

"What else do you want to watch, dude?" Rick asked as he went to pour another glass of vodka Coke.

"It's late for me. Do you mind if we go down to get my stuff from the car?" Steve asked.

"Holy shit, dude, did you leave your stuff in the car? We've got to haul ass. At this place, you can't leave nothin' in your car!" Rick said as he got his keys and rushed towards the door, with Steve following behind.

They trotted to the car, and to Steve's relief, everything was still there. Steve grabbed the suitcase, and Rick snagged Steve's computer bag.

"Dude, you are so fuckin' lucky. So fuckin' lucky!" Rick said as he shouldered the bag. "You don't leave anything in your car. In fact, don't even bother locking it. I had shit stolen from it all the time until I learned," Rick said.

But Steve knew Rick was a slow learner. "Thanks for the warning. I'll be careful."

Steve followed Rick through the maze that he was trying to memorize and back into Rick's apartment. When they entered, Rick turned around and locked the door.

"And dude, you always lock the door. I've got a spare key for you, but you always gotta lock the door. No exceptions. Leave for a second? Lock the door. Come inside to just take a piss? Lock the door. Capiche?" Rick said as he locked the second lock loudly to emphasize his meaning.

"Okay. Will do," Steve said, getting more tired by the minute.

"Here, dude, you can put your stuff over there. Just move my shit around," Rick said as he gestured towards an area near the sofa. "You can use this little table for your laptop."

Steve arranged his things as Rick brought him sheets and a blanket.

"I'll just head to my room and leave you to it. If you need to jack off, don't spurt it on the covers or the floor. Use a sock or some shit," Rick said as he laughed and closed the bedroom door.

Steve sat on the sofa. He silently took out his laptop, plugged it in, and sat it on the table. He pulled apart the sheets and blanket and made up the sofa as well as he could. He then sent a text to June.

"I'm doing okay. I'm staying at Rick's. Hope you have a good night!" He was trying to stay casual as if it were just another day.

After a few minutes, the three dots started dancing. June usually replied faster than this.

"Well, good. All is okay here. I told the kids you would be away for a little bit to work things out. Have a good sleep!" June replied, somewhat unemotionally.

Steve paused. "You too. Love you."

"I love you too, Steve," June responded. And that was that. He put the phone back down while tears welled in his eyes. He realized that he had finally—almost—reached rock bottom.

PART V

Days passed into weeks, and Steve was developing a routine. It wasn't the best routine, as his drinking continued, only to be joined with Rick's apparently endless supply of weed. Rick was a pot connoisseur. From Gorilla Glue IV to Sensi Star, Rick always had the good stuff. On occasion, he also bought some from the cannabis shops nearby, and Steve had even given him cash, so he didn't feel any more like the beggar than he already did. However, the store stuff didn't hold a candle to Rick's home-grown crops.

Rick had a great grow room, complete with carbon filters for the smell and an automatic watering system tied into the bathroom water supply line under the sink. When you went in there, it absolutely reeked of pot—a smell that Steve had oddly begun to enjoy. Outside the room, with the bottom of the door blocked and the carbon filter venting the pot-free air outside, even a police dog could not detect the odor. Rick was really a genius in some ways, but in the end, the apartment still smelled like pot and mildew from the smoking den, AKA the living room. Rick sometimes left the grow room door cracked a bit so the filter above the plants would draw the musty air out, but it didn't help much.

Steve flipped through the TV channels while Rick got ready to go out to his favorite bar to meet with his fellow degenerates. It was a true dive bar aptly called "The Dive." It was one of those bars that didn't have any windows or a single solid door. The type of door that was covered with old paper signs that had been taped into place and then ripped down, and the corners never removed. This, times one hundred other old paper signs, yellow with age and sunlight.

"Hey, loser, don't mess up the house or smoke all my weed," Rick said as he walked out the front door. Rick locked the door behind him out of habit, and Steve smiled, knowing that it was probably to protect his grow room rather than Steve.

Steve watched some bad TV and smoked weed. It was dark outside but still hot enough to wait a bit longer to go get some booze. The shows around this time of night were either movies that had already started or mindless sitcoms that Steve hated. Rick didn't have any streaming services as he put all his funds into weed, so TV was relegated to the olden days of thirteen channels of shit to choose from. True, there were about fifty channels on basic cable, but you could only watch the shopping networks for so long.

After the fifth rotation through the shows, Steve took a long last drag on his blunt and got up with a grunt to head out. He took his ID and some cash and slipped on his yellow Crocs. He left his cell phone on the kitchen counter so it wouldn't get stolen if he were mugged. As he stepped out and turned to lock the door, Steve paused.

"I don't have a knife. Shit!" he mumbled. Steve remembered what Rick said about the hood. While Rick talked smack on a regular basis, he wasn't wrong. This area was not entirely dangerous, but it also wasn't safe. It was unpredictable.

Steve walked back into the apartment and thought. He didn't want to take any of the kitchen knives, as carrying one in his pocket would be stupid. One hand placed in the wrong spot and that would be that. Steve shuddered at the thought.

As he walked around the room looking for something suitable for self-defense, Steve wandered into the grow room. After pausing to smell the plants, he noted a couple of pairs of pruning tools on Rick's workbench.

"That'll do nicely!" Steve said to himself. The sheers were top-of-the-line and quite sharp, with a hooked blade, perfect for trimming the juicy buds from the weed. They had a spring-loaded handle that locked into place while not in use, so when Steve put it into his right short's pocket, it remained closed and somewhat safe.

Steve headed back out the door, locked it as instructed, and started walking the mile or so to the store to get some vodka. While Steve wasn't as much of a drunk as he had been in his last days with June, he still drank enough for his liver to notice. Weed had replaced the alcohol enough to reduce his spending on "medicine," and it helped that Rick provided his weed for free.

The area was dark. What few streetlights there were had been vandalized, their copper wire stolen by the local druggies.

Although it was only a little after 11 p.m., there were very few people on the street.

Steve kept his head on a swivel as he used to do in Iraq. While he only did four years in the Army decades ago, there were still some habits that were so deeply embedded that he rarely noticed when he was doing them. With nobody behind him, Steve approached the canal near the store. Canals crisscrossed the city; they had been used to help distribute flood water and to act as irrigation. Now, they just smelled and collected shopping carts that the homeless mindlessly dropped into the water for reasons known only to the voices living in their heads.

Steve paused on the canal bridge to watch the trash float into the grate that was set to prevent larger items from migrating to the water treatment plant. The end result was a rolling undertow at the grate where larger pieces of trash were sucked down to the bottom of the canal, sort of how an alligator rolls and rolls as it kills its prey. Old cardboard used by a generation of homeless for shelter mixed with a mattress and unidentifiable waste was in a permanent state of motion in the rolling current. That is until the city dredged them once a year.

Steve turned the corner, still about five minutes away from the store. He thought about what to get as if he had a choice. His mind wandered with the memories of alcohol that actually tasted like something rather than just acid.

Steve finally reached the store and headed towards the vodka section. While he'd rather shop the scotch or rum aisle, his budget required the most basic of alcohol, which was indeed vodka. Steve had once toyed with the idea of going straight to Everclear grain alcohol. While it was 180 proof and cheap, he was afraid he'd wake up dead from overdoing it. While 100 proof was still strong, Steve knew his limit. He forgot this with June, of course.

Steve picked up two large bottles of booze and headed to the counter. The Indian who always worked the counter knew Steve by sight and nodded at him as he manually punched in the prices. The prices could vary by the day, but Steve and the man had an understanding that Steve's purchases would not vary, as the other customers did.

Over the shopkeeper's head was a video monitor that was split into several screens and clearly demonstrated that every corner of the store was under video surveillance. Not even a cockroach would be missed with the clarity of the cameras. It was interesting to Steve that there were no cameras outside, in part because they'd get stolen, but also, the owner didn't want to have to turn over any videos of the random crimes that happened on the street outside. Part selfishness, and part the liability of having something on video that could implicate the owner for knowing a crime happened that he didn't report. At least, that was the theory Steve held.

Steve handed over the cash and got his change. He dropped the coins into some nondescript donation box that was really a slush fund for the owner of the store. As he pocketed the dollars and took the double-bagged load of heavy vodka bottles, a group of at least six men walked boisterously into the store. They were the type of men who were full of false bravado and tended to act out to prove themselves to their fellow thugs. Not dangerous exactly, but unpredictable, and problematic if they focused on you.

Steve slowly walked out with the sole intention of bringing the least amount of attention to himself as possible. The bell at the door barked as Steve exited, and he coasted onto the sidewalk.

Having walked only fifty feet, Steve heard a man shout to him from the store.

"HEY, SHITHEAD! I KNOW YOU!" the man yelled.

Steve kept walking, trying to remain indifferent. He quickened his pace a bit, but not too much to be noticeable.

"Hey, fucktard, I'm talking to you!" the man said, now walking faster in a sort of trot to catch up with Steve. They were almost walking side by side within a few seconds.

"You're that fascist shithead from that restaurant video! You are that fucking white supremacist!" he blurted, only a few feet from Steve's ears.

Steve kept walking as they turned the corner, heading towards the canal. He shifted the bag of alcohol to his left hand and quickened his pace more. His mind raced as fast as his legs did, while outwardly, he was displaying calmness.

"I'm glad I ruined your life, you shit. Assholes like you think they can walk around and fuck over my people, you privileged shit!" his aggressor spat.

Steve glanced over to look at the man. His mind reeled through his memories until he connected the dots and recognized the man as Frankie, also known as @FrankieGTHollywood. Frankie's profile picture and the endless videos of him doing randomly stupid pranks to the unsuspecting would forever be in Steve's mind. His pompadour yellow-green hair was the clincher. Steve also looked behind him. Frankie's friends were nowhere to be seen.

"Leave me alone," Steve said in a low, quiet voice. His hand moved into his right pocket, and he fingered the sheers to make sure they were still there. They were nearing the canal as Frankie leaned in closer.

"FUCK IF I WILL, YOU SHIT!" Frankie screamed into his ear. "YOU GOT WHAT YOU DESERVED!"

Steve put his hand around the sheers in his pocket and kept on walking as quickly as his Crocs would allow. At this point, Steve just hoped that Frankie would get bored talking to a wall.

"You got what you deserved, and so did that bitch wife of yours. Maybe it's time to cancel your daughter too!" Frankie hissed.

Something snapped in Steve. He slowed his pace and removed the sheers from his pocket. He swung his arm around, using the bottles of vodka as a counterbalance, and thrust the clippers into Frankie's neck below his left ear.

"LEAVE US ALONE!" Steve bellowed as the sheers popped into Frankie's neck, like shoving a toothpick into Jell-O.

Frankie screamed a muffled gasp and started to bend down to get away from Steve's hand and whatever he'd been stabbed with. Steve looked into his eyes and saw both surprise and fear.

He grabbed the front of Frankie's shirt with his left hand and held it tight, the bottles clanking and acting as a weight around Frankie's neck. The clippers' top blade had pierced down to the hinge. The bottom blade was starting to slice a groove in Frankie's skin.

Frankie started to panic even more as he tried to pull away from Steve's grasp on his shirt and the sheers in his neck.

Steve held Frankie tightly and, with the sheers in his neck, began to dig, clipping and scissoring through the soft tissue, only to meet some resistance when they snipped his jugular before exiting from behind Frankie's Adam's apple.

Frankie gurgled a sickening slurp of blood as it simultaneously flooded his lungs and spurted out in a ribbon of dark red that sprayed onto Steve's face, then cascaded into the open bag that held the vodka and over his Crocs.

Steve pushed Frankie away from his chest, and he collapsed into a fetal position while the remaining blood pulsed out onto the grass by the sidewalk. Frankie was now silent as he pulsed and shuddered and finally died.

Steve froze for a moment while the adrenaline coursed through his body. He started to shake. The salty iron of the atomized blood spray dripped from Steve's mouth. He bent down and spit out what he could and used his blood-soaked shirt to wipe the red fluid from his face.

"Oh, fuck me!" Steve mumbled. As he rose, he looked around. He couldn't see anyone else, and the area where they fought was fairly dark. He carefully put his vodka bag on the ground. It held about a quart of thickening blood, which covered the bottles. He looked around again, with fear now adding to his cascading anger that had ended Frankie. Steve had seen a lot of things while in Iraq for Operation Desert Storm, and he had even been part of a few hut breaches that ended in bloodshed. But this was the most blood Steve had ever seen, and his balls tightened.

"Got to hide him! Gotta hide him!" Steve mumbled, eyeing the canal. Dragging Frankie backward with his legs, he pulled him through the grass between the sidewalk and the street. As he neared the canal, Steve changed his path to walk through the dirt by the edge.

He straightened out Frankie and laid his body parallel to the canal. With one large push, he rolled him in. Frankie rolled limply into the water and entered with the most minor of splashes. Steve watched in horror as Frankie's body floated just below the surface of the water.

"Oh, fuck me twice!" Steve whispered again. He looked around and behind him. Near an abandoned building was a shopping cart. Stolen shopping carts littered the area, so this one wouldn't be missed. Steve wheeled it down to the canal embankment and positioned it over Frankie's floating body, hoping beyond hope that this plan would work. He pushed the cart onto its side and on top of the corpse, which finally sank the body.

Steve watched for a few more minutes as the water churned near the grate, which was now the final resting place for the troll.

"Fuck 'em, the fucker," Steve murmured as he went back to pick up his bag. Still shaking, he took the bottles out to empty the blood from the bag. He was horrified to see that the blood was now like silly putty and remained in the bag. Steve wretched from the smell of burnt pennies as he put the bottles back into the bag with a squish and walked back to the apartment. He walked slowly enough to appear to be without a care in the world, but his blood-covered clothes made him look like either a murder victim or a killer.

Steve made it back into the apartment and locked the door. He went to the kitchen and removed the vodka once again. He put the plastic bags into a large Ziplock bag that Rick kept for his larger bundles of pot. He sealed the Ziplock and stuffed it into the kitchen trash as deep as possible into the middle of a mass of rotten pizza and who knows what else. Steve washed the bottles, his hands, his face, his hair, and his Crocs over and over for thirty minutes as he stood at the sink in shock. He stripped and put the bloody clothes into the washer, added two cups of bleach, and started its cycle. Now naked, Steve sat down in Rick's chair with his elbows on his knees and stared at the carpet.

Just moments later, Rick unlocked the door and staggered in, obviously drunk. Steve looked up at Rick and then back down.

"What the freaky fuckity fuck is this, Steve?" Rick said as he walked towards a naked Steve. He was almost catatonic as Rick moved him to the couch and covered him up. "No more pot for you for a while, you stupid shit!"

Lying on the couch, Steve's mind raced for hours until he finally fell asleep to dreams of Frankie screaming like a bunny being killed by a coyote. Steve was the coyote.

PART VI

Steve woke up to one of those moments where the curtain between a dream and reality seemed thinner; it was difficult to know which was which. He opened his eyes, and his stomach immediately sank as he realized that what seemed like a dream had, in fact, happened. Frankie had pushed all the right buttons to drive Steve to attack, and Steve was as surprised as Frankie was when he lashed out.

"I'm so fucked. Fuck me, fuck me. FUCK ME!" Steve blurted. Rick had already gone to work, so he was alone. There were no witnesses to Steve's despair.

He lay on the sofa, staring at the smoke-stained ceiling and reliving the previous night's mayhem. As he racked his brain and memory for anything that he could have done differently, Steve's mind shifted to the now.

He turned on the television and flitted between as many local stations as he could find. Some channels were still on their morning show segments. He picked the newsiest channel and passively watched it, anticipating and dreading seeing a story about a body found in the canal. Steve was pretty sure that the blood had mostly ended up in the grass, so there would not be much to find on the ground where Steve eliminated… murdered… Frankie. After an hour, he had seen nothing. No mention of a body. No blurry videos of Steve slicing Frankie's neck. Nothing.

Steve eventually got up and methodically went through his morning routine. It consisted of a good shit followed by a short shower. This time, he spent twice as long in the shower making sure he didn't miss anything that shouldn't still be there and incriminate him if the police burst through the door. As he dried off with the last clean towel, he suddenly remembered the clothes in the washer. Naked, he went into the little room that held the washer and dryer and peered inside to see the results of the wash.

Steve's clothes were a bit brighter, but that only stood to highlight the remaining blood stains, and there were a lot.

"Oh, fuck me!" he blurted, suddenly remembering more about the night as the taste and smell of the blood hit him. Frankie's gurgle. The way his body was pulled down by the shopping cart…

Thinking about what to do next, his stomach tossing, Steve went to put on fresh clothes. His Crocs had already been thoroughly washed in the sink in the panic of the aftermath of the killing. He put them on and paced.

"I've got to get rid of these clothes!" Steve said to himself, then pulled out a trash bag and loaded it with the contents of the washer. He put the bag into two more trash bags and tied each one tightly in succession. Now, with a mostly sealed bag of bloody clothes, he sat in Rick's chair to think. The constant turning of his stomach didn't help.

Deciding he needed to do something, anything, he grabbed his keys and wallet and took the bag out to the car. He purposefully left his cell phone in the apartment to avoid being tracked. And for good reason. While Steve didn't have his phone when he killed Frankie, he didn't want to start a trail of him disposing of evidence.

He unlocked his car, slumped inside, and placed the bag behind the passenger seat so as to appear normal—if that could be possible. He could say it was a Salvation Army donation if stopped.

"Okay, now what, you fucking criminal?" Steve rhetorically asked himself. He sat for a moment to work out where might be the best place to dump the bag, somewhere it couldn't be traced back to the crime. Eventually, he decided upon an apartment dumpster. They were everywhere, emptied regularly, and all kinds of trash were thrown in them. Broken chairs, toys, and bags of dirty diapers all formed the toxic mix of your average apartment dumpster.

Having disabled the GPS in his car to further avoid detection, Steve wanted to stick to routes he already knew as he was quite directionally challenged. Fortunately, most of the roads in the Phoenix area formed a grid, and he would be able to cross between cities without noticing. And the individual municipal police departments didn't communicate as well as they should. Steve picked Glendale as the target city and made his way to the poorer ends of town. Of course, this was Glendale, so most of the city was poor.

Steve found a sprawling apartment complex and navigated to a dumpster deep inside the maze of parking. The dumpster was huge and only half full. It reeked of mold, diapers, and despair. He could smell it from over twenty feet away.

He sat in the car for over an hour to survey the area before casually tossing in a few pieces of decoy trash he had in the trunk, along with the bag. Finished, he walked back to the car and pulled out of the parking lot. Steve was relatively sure that most of the doors in this complex didn't have doorbell cameras and that any surveillance by the management wasn't focused on the dumpsters but on the rampant drug use and prostitution that permeated the neighborhood.

On the drive back to Rick's apartment, Steve listened to a talk radio station that had local news every thirty minutes. Stomach churning, His anxiety was reaching a peak as the 11:30 a.m. news approached.

The main story was about a protest near the State Capital and focused on sound bites from each side.

"Get the fuck on with it!" he hissed.

The second story featured a new strip mall that featured Bolivian food and merch. Still nothing about Frankie.

He parked at Rick's apartment and slumped in his seat. The tightness in his balls and the tickle in his stomach slowly subsided as he sat contemplating the situation at hand. He had murdered someone and disposed of the evidence. Apparently, successfully, he mused.

"Maybe I dodged that bullet," Steve whispered to himself as he left the car, making sure to lock it and then double-checked that it was indeed locked as Rick had warned him.

As he walked to the apartment, Steve looked around for any law enforcement. The coast was clear, and he sighed as he unlocked the door and went inside. His cell phone was still sitting on the kitchen table and showed five new messages. Each was from June.

He picked up his phone and held it against his forehead, not yet capable of reading the messages. As the warmth of the phone reached his skin, Steve sighed. He lowered his phone and quietly wept as he made his replies.

CHAPTER THREE

"This is the most awesome video! It's not fun and games anymore, is it, Kathy? AKA Baby Fascist. Run you loser. Run back to your fascist daddy!!!"

Amber Hardy (@AHardOne)

PART I

Steve awoke from a fitful sleep and stared at the ceiling. Although he had only just finished disposing of the evidence of his crime, he still had a bit of an uplifted spirit. He had chatted with June a lot the previous night and even texted a bit with the kids. Although they were fully Gen Z, they texted worse than an old cat lady with emojis.

Steve got up stiffly and took a shower. The warm water felt good as it flowed over his head and down his back, washing away the guilt.

As the water started to turn cold, he turned it off and dried himself with a mildly dirty towel. Steve mumbled that he really needed to wash his blankets and towel and maybe hide them from Rick, who had an ongoing issue of dirt and grime that permeated the apartment. Quite the opposite of his grow room.

"Hey, fucknugget, see your sorry ass later. Unlike your lazy butt, I've got a job!" Rick chortled as he left and promptly locked the door behind him.

Steve thought about this, and perhaps, maybe, indeed, it was time to look for a job. He'd have to cut down on drinking and smoking Rick's stash, but maybe it was time. Steve and June had been chatting more during his more lucid moments, and this seemed like an improvement.

As he poured himself a vodka margarita, his phone jumped alive. It was Kathy's ringtone. The first time he had heard it since The Day.

Steve answered the phone and was greeted with a sobbing scream.

"DADDY, THEY'RE AFTER ME!" Kathy blurted with fear in her voice. "They found me, and now this guy is following me and bumping my car! What do I do?"

Steve's forehead veins instantly popped as he struggled to understand what was happening.

"Kathy, listen closely. You need to drive to someplace crowded right now, and hang up with me and call 911. Do it now!" Steve instructed, with unconstrained anger in his voice. "Call me back after you call 911!" The phone went dead.

Steve paced back and forth for what seemed to be an eternity. Thoughts raced through his head as he took some big slugs of his vodkarita.

He picked up his phone, opened Chatter, and searched for Kathy. He hadn't used the app since The Day, mainly for avoidance and also, more recently, to avoid any trigger that may excite him to the extent he would repeat, well, The Frankie Event.

Finding Kathy, he searched her timeline of replies. Nothing. Then he just searched for her handle. @KatMeow24 brought forth dozens of results. Steve scrolled through them and the rage filled him quickly. Some user named @AHardOne put out a call to dox Kathy as she'd spotted her in Steve's Marisol video. Somehow, her followers did some facial recognition using a free online app and tracked her down. From there, it was a series of hateful posts and calls for some type of unspecified revenge… for something. Anything. They had found her last name and posted her address, as they'd matched it up with Steve's public property records combined with some additional facial identification. Someone had stalked her at Steve's house and posted a photo of Kathy's license plate. From there, the harassment just got worse.

Steve continued to scroll through the responses, revenge filling his thoughts. How could anyone do this for no reason? It was a foreign concept to Steve, although he had already experienced it himself, which had led to his current situation. However, now the mob had fucked with the wrong person.

Steve jumped as his phone came alive with Kathy's ringtone. It had been nearly ten minutes.

"Daddy, I'm okay," Kathy said, somewhat out of breath. "I stayed on the line with the operator, and a cop showed up next to me. But the guy drove away. They didn't get him, Daddy!"

"It's okay, I'm sure he won't try that again, whoever he was," Steve said, fury clouding his mind.

"They were so nice and had me keep reading what street names I passed. I actually stayed calm!" Kathy exclaimed with ragged breaths, proud of her composure.

"Well, I'm glad you were so brave and strong! Great job!" Steve said. Again, with a raging monster yelling behind his eyeballs.

"Daddy, when are you coming back? We really miss you. Mom cries almost every day. Even Brian misses you, but he can't tell you that," Kathy said.

Steve's eyes filled with tears at the words, but he held back and kept his voice calm. "I'll be home soon, sweetie. I'm working things out, and I'm even starting to look for another job! I'll get things sorted and ask your mother if I can come back home."

Kathy sighed. "I hope so. I know I was sometimes a bit of a bitch before, and I'm so sorry. I really miss you!"

Steve welled up even more. "I miss you too, sweetie. I'll be home soon. Remember, if you need anything, call me. Right?"

Steve could hear Kathy's nodding over the phone. "I will, Daddy. I love you,"

"I love you too, sweetie," Steve said before pressing the end button. His mind was racing. He opened his phone again to read the message that started these problems for his beautiful, innocent daughter. *"This is the most awesome video! It's not fun and games anymore, is it, Kathy? AKA Baby Fascist. Run you loser. Run back to your fascist daddy!!!"* Amber Hardy (@AHardOne)

"Amber is done. She's fucking done!" Steve muttered with rage, his body vibrating in anger.

PART II

S teve spent the better part of two days stalking Amber online and making a spider chart of all the people that she had rallied to dox Kathy. Surprisingly, Amber lived in Phoenix and worked at a local coffee shop. *How convenient.*

One of the most boisterous voices in the chatter was Michelle, Steve's former coworker. As @Michelada911, Michelle had been quite active in disparaging Steve and Kathy. Her stories about Steve's former work life were complete fiction but showed just how much Michelle despised Steve for whatever reason.

"Congratulations, Michelle. You made the list," Steve mumbled as he continued to map the network of users. As Steve had finally reached what seemed to be the end of the list of co-conspirators, he focused on Amber and who her closest friends were in real life. Those she met up with and the places she went. Amber led a full life. She spent it between her job as a barista and going to various bars and sporting events. Her core group seemed to really be into sports. Not really to see the sport, but to be seen. They mostly got drunk, did stupid things, and documented it all on a variety of social media platforms.

As Steve scrolled, Rick arrived home with his usual bluster.

"Hey, asswipe! What a shitty day I had. Michelle is on the warpath! That bitch reported me to HR again. I just called her a thundercunt, and she got all bent. I got a write-up, and it's basically my final boo-boo," Rick pouted as he flopped into his chair.

Steve pondered. "What are you going to do?"

"Fuck if I know. I'll just keep quiet for a few weeks, and it will blow over. Then maybe I'll get reported for being too quiet. You know, like a ticking time bomb? You can't fucking win sometimes, dude!" Rick said as he lit up a pre-rolled doobie.

"You know it," Steve mumbled as he took a hit from Rick's smoke. "You know it."

Steve pondered a bit more. "Hey, what would you do if someone came after your daughter online? As in real life?"

"Man, I'd fuck them up good. Did someone bother Kathy? That's your daughter's name, right? Kathy?" Rick said as he blew out a cloud of aerosol pot smoke.

"Yeah, that's her name. Nah, nothing has happened. I was just thinking, what if?" Steve said.

Rick leaned back into his chair and pontificated. "Yeah, man, I'd fucking kill them quicker than shit. They'd be done. Like most of the people that plague this world." As he trailed off, he slowly shut his eyes as if to fantasize about what he would do.

The night moved along, and the pot and vodka flowed. Steve slowly began to plot and plan. As he drifted off to sleep, his mind was filled with Kathy's crying.

PART III

It was finally Friday, and Rick rolled out of his room to get a cup of coffee before he headed in to make a silent battle with Michelle.

"What in the ever-loving fuckity fuck have you done to yourself, fucking Pink Floyd!" Rick blurted when he entered the room to see Steve was hairless.

"Like my new look? I got tired of my hair, so it's gone," Steve said.

Rick stared at Steve. "Holy shit, even your fucking eyebrows? You look like a fucking freak!"

"Maybe I like it? What's not to like?" Steve mused as he rubbed his bald head, enjoying its surprising smoothness. It had taken him a bit to get it all off, but once done, it was done. There was no turning back. And it made DNA matching more difficult. It was a win-win.

"Man, you do you, you freak. Catch you later, Pink," Rick said, then picked up his coffee and headed to the door. With a snap of the lock, he was gone.

Steve sat down on the sofa and pulled up Amber. Tonight, she and her friends were excited about going to the Diamondback's baseball game. All kinds of hashtags and emojis flowed between her and her two BFFs.

"I'll be seeing you soon, Amber. Wish you well!" Steve murmured as he scrolled.

- 142 -

PART IV

Afternoon came, and Steve arrived at the ballpark by 4 p.m. The pedicabs were starting to bustle for a good place to take people to the game. Steve watched as they parked, and some then left their rides by the curb while they grabbed a beer (or five) in the nearby bars. One stood out in particular: a chain-driven cab with a large, single back seat big enough to hold three. He waited for the cabbie to go inside before he took the cycle and rode off to his hiding spot.

Steve had walked to the game from Rick's apartment. It was a grueling walk, especially in Crocs, which made it infinitely more difficult. But, from personal experience, Crocs were easy to clean.

He carried a backpack with his water, bleach, a plastic sheet, a sign for Amber, and his knife. He had gotten the knife from Amazon using a gift card that he paid cash for. He had gotten it dropped off in a locker to avoid it being tracked to Rick's place. He had also left his phone behind when he did.

The knife was a full 10 inches long and resembled a British WWII paratrooper knife. It was really almost a dagger. Again, without his cell phone, he had actually printed out a map like they did in the olden days to make it to the game. He didn't want to even check the address on the phone, so with the old-school map, he worked out it would take three hours to walk there, and it pretty much did.

As Steve waited for the game to start, he prepared the pedicab with the plastic sheet and positioned the bleach on the floorboard. After the initial crowds began to thin out, all taking their seats in the stadium, he checked his phone and worked out Amber was going to arrive late to the game and would be driving alone.

"How the turns have tabled!" Steve mumbled an old dad joke as he watched the comments come in. Amber's friends were asking her to hurry and pick up some beers from the concessions on her way to their seats.

As the innings passed and the game wrapped up, Steve was fully up-to-date on where their seats were and, therefore, what exit they would use. He pulled up to the curb and waited. He had watched their drunken antics in near real-time.

The crowd started to flow out of the exits and quickly became an army of ants, moving like an organic swarm. Steve finally saw Amber and the gang stumble out of the gate. One of the girls was absolutely fall-down drunk, and it took a bit for Amber to extract herself after much arm flapping. Finally, she headed over to the pedicab line. As Amber got closer, Steve pulled out the cardboard sign with her name on it. And so began the end of Amber.

PART V

A mber was dead. Just before her end, Steve had some sympathy for her while she gasped and sprayed the last of her blood onto the plastic. It was quickly dismissed. She deserved it, even if it was a bit more gruesome than he had expected. Nobody fucks with Steve's family.

"Sorry, Amber. You brought this upon yourself," Steve mumbled while Amber's neck still oozed blood.

Letting go, he let her fall onto the floor. Panting from the effort and drenched in sweat, he then drove the completely operable pedicab into a dead alley. The chain break was fiction. Theatrical swerving, breaking, and reversing the peddling was convincing enough.

As he sat to collect himself and to reflect on what he did, he realized that it wasn't as traumatic as the first one. His adrenalin was coursing, to be sure, but his daughter was now rid of her altogether. He'd take care of the rest if he needed to, starting with Michelle.

He laid the plastic sheeting on the ground next to Amber and rolled her on top of it. He poured most of the bottle of bleach onto her body, especially around her head where he had grabbed her. The bleach wasn't watered down, and the smell of blood mixed with the sanitizer was horrific. He gagged as he rolled her up in the plastic with the Amber sign he had used and then schlepped her body wrapped like a burrito to the dumpster. He pushed her over and in, laying Amber in her grave.

Steve sat for a few seconds, then got the rest of the bleach and poured it over the pedicab handlebars and then onto his hands. He wrung his hands out with the bleach and cursed as it started to burn. His bottle of cheap Costco water helped remove some of the sting.

Out of his pocket, he picked up a Ziploc bag with a small piece of paper inside. On the paper was a screenshot of one of Amber's most liked posts about another poor soul who had enraged Amber's sensibilities about some minor perceived infraction. She had doxed that target, too and had also gotten them fired. It seemed like it was her part-time job.

Steve dropped the paper with the screenshot onto the pedicab's passenger seat and let it fall as it may, without touching it. He had already prepared it with gloves and tweezers and had wiped the bag down with bleach earlier in the day.

He put the empty baggie into his pocket and began the three-hour walk in the dark back to Rick's place. He fingered the knife in his pocket; it was, after all, a bad part of town. Steve only added to the vibe as a participant.

CHAPTER FOUR

"I've worked with this asshole, and I can assure you that everything is true and worse. He was an ass to everyone he worked with and especially hates women. He deserves to be canceled if anyone ever did!"

Michelle Connor (@Michelada911)

PART I

Steve awoke with a start. He had arrived back at Rick's place around 2 a.m. and crept in without a sound. He locked the door behind him, of course, and Rick never woke up from his pot fugue. Steve had dropped off the knife in Rick's apartment dumpster after pulling out some trash and wrapping it up in a mixture of diapers and fast-food bags.

He had repeated his clean-up by putting his clothes in a double bag, bleaching his shoes, and making the trek to his favorite apartment complex to dump the evidence. His phone, naturally, stayed behind.

Rick had already left for the day while Steve was sleeping, and that left Steve to stare at the ceiling. He had come to grips with what he had done, and while the tinge of remorse lingered, his thoughts went to his daughter. She was still in danger.

Steve turned on his phone, and six messages and three missed phone calls popped into life. June had obviously been trying to get in touch, and Steve called her immediately.

June answered the phone and blurted out. "You know what happened to Kathy, right? Yes?"

"She phoned me when some stalker tried to follow her. What's happened now?" Steve asked frantically.

"It's happened again, just this time she didn't see it. Someone was outside our house taking pictures of MY car! Can you make this stop, Steve? CAN YOU?" June pleaded, her voice rising in pitch with her emotions.

Steve sat in silence. His mind raced on what to say to June. "I'll make it stop. Don't worry."

"How? Just how will you make it stop?" she asked, the anguish still in her voice.

"Don't worry about it. I'll handle it," he said.

June started to cry. It broke Steve's heart.

"I want you back home soon. Do you hear me?" June sobbed.

"I'm looking for a job, and I'm getting sober," Steve lied. He hated lying, especially with a drink in his hand. He just wasn't ready to let go, and that bothered him.

"Get it together and come home. We all miss you. We need you," June said, starting to settle down.

"I love you. I'll be back to my old self soon. I promise," Steve said, downing his drink.

June sighed. "I love you too, Steve. Bye-bye."

The line clicked, and June was gone. Steve sat down, poured himself another drink, and settled on the sofa. He pulled up his research on Michelle and started to map out her contacts.

PART II

It was Friday, and Steve began his three-hour walk downtown to finally meet Michelle again in person. The Phoenix City Hall was near the ballpark, and Steve knew the walk well. He had his backpack with his bleach, water, a surgical mask, vodka, and a new knife. This time, it was a serrated blade K-Bar style knife—Also known as the preferred fighting knife of the Marine Corps. It was quite common, and the cuts it made were gruesome.

He made his way by the canals and down the street. He had preloaded with two stadium cups of vodkaritas, but a swig from his handled bottle of vodka kept him at the proper level of smashed. Fortunately, the bottle got lighter with each drink as he neared downtown.

Arriving at the parking garage around 4 p.m., Steve put his mask on and pretended like he was just another homeless person.

Steve already knew where all the surveillance cameras were and knew that there were none inside the garage itself. And with this in mind, Steve walked into the pedestrian entrance, shuffling as he went. He had procured a grocery store cart and put some trash in it to cover his backpack, completing the image.

Parking his cart inside the garage, Steve walked up the ramps to where Michelle consistently parked. The stairs were in view of the cameras across the street, so the ramps were a safer bet to remain unseen. Once Steve found Michelle's car, he walked in between it and the one next to it and scuttled under.

He was alarmed to find that he almost didn't fit. The car was lower than expected, and the claustrophobia sat in almost immediately. He was expecting to wait two hours for Michelle's normal departure time of 6 p.m., and the fit made it truly uncomfortable.

Right on schedule, he saw Michelle's high heels clicking as she walked toward her car. She was one of the few employees who stayed until six o'clock on a Friday. The garage had pretty much cleared out, and there were only a few cars left on the fifth floor.

Michelle walked to the driver's door, and Steve heard the beeps of the car unlocking. With his right hand, he slid out the K-Bar and, in one complete motion, cut Michelle's Achilles to the bone.

Michelle immediately fell to the ground, and Steve reached out and covered her mouth the best he could with his free hand. It slipped, and Michelle started to scream out, her eyes bugging in surprise and fear. Steve wiggled his body out from under the car and dragged Michelle headfirst onto his lap, and then he slumped against the garage wall. Being exposed, Steve held her tight against him with her head at chin level and worked fast.

"Hey there, Michelle! It's Steve. How ya doing?" Steve whispered, his hand now covering her mouth harder and his knife resting on her chest so she could see it.

Michelle tried to wriggle out of Steve's grasp but stopped when the knife was put point first on her breast.

"Did you think that you could just destroy my life and threaten my family without consequences? You're such a fucking cold bitch, you know that?"

Michelle mumbled and cried and shook her head no as she seemed to surrender to what was happening.

"I'm going to lower my hand and let you whisper. Do you hear me? If you scream, I will cut your heart out so fast that when I force you to eat it, you will taste it before you die. Do you understand? Nod your head yes if you understand," Steve hissed.

Michelle nodded her head in the affirmative, so Steve lowered his hand and let it rest on her throat, gripping it tightly.

"I'm sorry, Steve, I'm so sorry, don't kill me! I'm so sorry!" Michelle whispered, sobbing through the words.

"That's it? You're sorry? How insulting. You've threatened my family and had your followers do the same." Steve said.

Michelle shuddered and cried harder as Steve moved his hand back to her mouth. Michelle mumbled something between his fingers, and Steve spread them to let her speak.

"Hank died a few months ago. You know he had cancer. Our daughter only has me! Please don't kill me!" Michelle begged.

Steve's mind thrashed at her words. "Fuck me," he whispered. He couldn't let her go, or they'd pin the other murders on him within days. The anguish going through his mind was absolutely disabling. But this was a point of no return, and Steve's family was in danger.

"I'm sorry, Michelle. I know your parents are still alive and will take care of her. As you die, know that she will be okay. Oh, and Rick sends his regards," Steve whispered into her ear, his spittle dancing on her neck. Spittle and tears.

Michelle and Steve both sobbed silently as Steve shoved the knife through her rib cage and into her heart. He twisted it as it went in, and he heard a strange crackle of bone. Steve was careful not to go all the way through her so he didn't also impale himself.

"I'm so sorry. I'm so sorry!" Steve cried uncontrollably as Michelle stiffened and weakly flailed her arms and legs in pain as the blood pooled out of the wound and onto her chest and lap.

A few moments later, Michelle was dead. Steve extricated himself from beneath her body by pushing it off his lap, then rolled it under the car. He used the bleach to saturate the pavement and remove some of the blood streaks as he began to shake. "Fuck, fuck, fuck, fuck!" he hissed. "I'm so sorry. Oh God, I'm so sorry."

He was surprisingly horrified at how this had gone. It was so much more personal than he had ever expected. His stomach dropped out of his bowels, and his balls tightened and burned as he ruminated on Michelle's cries for her daughter.

He removed the baggie with the clipping from one of Michelle's posts about somebody else that she had trolled and placed it under the car. Steve hoped that this would lead the police to a dead end for at least a bit. Her body would be found as it started to smell, but at least that might not be until Monday.

With everything tidied up, Steve noticed that he was surprisingly free of a lot of Michelle's blood, as it had mostly soaked into her clothes. This didn't take away the horror that he felt at leaving a child an orphan, not like the others, where revenge seemed justified or even appropriate.

Steve pulled himself off the ground and headed back down the parking garage ramp. He mumbled to himself as he walked away, unknowingly leaving a partial imprint of his Crocs behind.

CHAPTER FIVE

"Phoenix Police is aware of a series of killings that appear to have a common thread. The perpetrator, who we're calling the "Chatter Killer," targeted specific people based on posts that the victims allegedly made. More information to follow."

Phoenix Police PIO (@PhxPolice)

PART I

Steve woke up the following morning, still wearing the clothes from the night before. With minimal blood to deal with, Steve had drunk another handle of vodka before passing out into a dreamless sleep on Rick's sofa.

Awakening hours later, he found Rick had already left for work, leaving Steve in his misery. The murder had, for once, hit home. It wasn't just about revenge. Or justice. Steve thought for the first time that he had crossed a line in his rage and entered the realm of a serial killer. The anguish was unbearable.

He put his clothes into his standard evidence disposal trash bag for later and took a shower. As he reflected under the running water, his mind flashed back to the murder. It was an experience that would prove to be impossible to get over, for both Steve and Michelle.

After drying himself with a dirty towel from Rick's bathroom floor, Steve picked up his cell phone and turned it back on. He had six text messages from June and two missed calls from her. He hung up the towel and went into the living room to call June.

"Where were you, Steve?" June asked, with a small tremor in her voice. "I'm so very worried about you."

Steve thought quickly and murmured out a believable explanation of being asleep. June seemed to calm down. For a moment, Steve thought that maybe June really did want him back.

"How are the kids? How's Kathy?" Steve asked.

June hesitated for a moment. "I think she's doing better. The posts have calmed down a bit, so that's good."

"Yes, that is good," Steve agreed while thinking of Michelle and her child.

"Do you think you'll be coming home soon? I could really do with hearing your silly jokes again," June said.

Steve felt his stomach erupt with a swarm of butterflies. Maybe June DID want him back.

"Give me a couple of weeks so I can start my new job. Is that okay?" Steve lied. Although he had been to a few interviews, nothing had hit yet. He had even stopped drinking for a few hours to appear somewhat put together for the video interviews.

"Take the time you need, honey. I just need you home. The kids do, too. They need their sober father back."

June's comment struck home, as Steve hadn't been sober in months. He had tried drinking less but found that to do so carried its own consequences. He had almost gotten used to the inflamed and painful pancreas. While the alcohol caused it, it also took the pain away for a while.

"I'm doing my best, and I promise that when I come back home, it will be for good. No drinking. I didn't use to be a heavy drinker, and I can be that way again. I was in a very dark place," Steve said. Now, it was his voice that was quivering.

June, sensing that Steve was sincere, agreed. She remembered those days, and while nobody is perfect, Steve had always tried to be the best father and husband.

"I know, honey. It's okay. We've all been impacted by this series of fucking stupid events," she replied.

Steve was shocked at June's cursing. Now he realized how deep the well was in her anger. And the depths that she had gone to deal with it.

Steve and June said their goodbyes, and he then sat in silence and stared at Rick's blank walls for over an hour.

"I'm done. I'm done with this shit, and I'm done with you!" Steve suddenly yelled, glaring at the empty vodka bottles lining the countertop. If an inanimate object could feel shame, it was now. Although the bottles didn't seem to react, Steve continued to glare.

He waited to get off the couch until Rick got home from running Saturday errands. His mind had been reeling from his conversation with June and Michelle's murder. For the first time, a feeling of dread crept into his thinking as he now faced the real possibility that he would go home, only to be taken away to prison. At least he would be sober.

"What's up, fuckwad?" Rick asked. "You just been pimping on my sofa all day?"

"I need a favor, Rick," Steve said.

Rick suddenly stopped in his tracks and faced Steve.

"Anything, buddy. Anything! What do you need?" Rick asked, his brow furrowed. For somebody as cracked as Rick, he did have an honest and kind side to him.

"I'm sober now. As of now. As of right now. Can you help me? Just watch me," Steve pleaded, tears forming in the corners of his eyes.

"Well, you have been partaking quite a bit, my friend. Why the change?" Rick said.

"I need to go home, and I can't do it and drink too. I'm done," Steve replied.

Rick laughed and said, "Well, I do need you to get your ass off my couch, ya loser! Just tell me what you need me to do."

Steve pondered the request for a moment. "Just watch me. I don't know what will happen, but just watch me. I'm going to stay right here. Can you get me water when I need it? And no matter what happens, DO NOT call June and DO NOT take me to a hospital." Steve wanted to avoid the hospital and any questions. He couldn't do in-patient rehab. Not enough time.

"Okay, dude. Whatever you want, you cray-cray dumbass. This might not go well for you to just go cold turkey," Rick said, eyeing Steve with an overdone skeptical eye. "But I'll do it. Just this once. No redos."

"Thanks, Rick. You have no idea how much I appreciate this," Steve whispered sincerely.

"Thank me now, dumbass. You'll curse me later," Rick replied.

PART II

The following week was a living hell for Steve. He had expected mental depression and maybe even a bit of the delirium tremors he had heard about. This was not the case at all.

After days of violent shaking and seizures, Steve remained glued to the sofa in various stages of unconsciousness. Rick stayed by Steve's side like a caring dad and kept him hydrated the best he could. He had finally given up on getting Steve to the bathroom and went to the store to pick up some adult diapers.

"I didn't have changing a grown man's panties on my bingo card this year," Rick said to himself. Steve was unconscious.

Days passed, and as he recovered, scenes of the murders came and went through Steve's head with alternating feelings of fear and dread. In his few waking moments, he realized that he was covered in sweat and smelled terrible, like a mixture of urine, blood, and yeast. But soon, Steve sat up.

Rick walked in to see Steve in an upright position. "Hey, dipshit! You back?"

"Yeah. I think so. Can I have some juice?" Steve asked as a sudden feeling of light-headedness took over. He reached up to rub his head and hopefully massage away the raging headache that had melted his brain. A new field of hair had popped up. He knew at this point that he had been out for more than just a few days. His stubble also verified the passage of time, and that bothered Steve.

"I have some of your old margarita mix but no juice," Rick said, making a pruned face.

"No, thanks, dude. No thanks. Can I just have some water, then? Maybe a cracker? Hey, how long was I out?" Steve asked.

Rick seemed to ignore him and went over to get a stadium-sized cup of water and a half-empty sleeve of crackers.

"Here you go, bud," Rick said as he handed Steve the water. "You've been a shaking vegetable for almost a week. A veg covered in sweat, piss, and shit. You were a wreck, dude!"

Steve downed the entire glass and ate a few crackers. Who knows what damage he had done to his body during his detox. At least it might be better than what he had already done, minus the murders, of course. He had damaged a few other bodies in his fit of anger and theoretical justice.

Rick suddenly came to attention as he remembered something. "Hey, dude, you want to hear something really fucked up? Guess!" He was tip-tapping in place like a toy dog.

"Dude, I'm so tired," Steve said, slumping just a bit.

"Don't be a weak pussy. No, man, for real, Michelle got herself killed! Right in the parking garage. Shit, man, I even parked close to where her car was. How fucked up is that crazy shit?" Rick said.

A shock went through Steve's mind, and he immediately yearned for a drink.

"Dude, that is fucked up," Steve replied. "Do they know who did it?"

Rick walked over to sit in his recliner and light up a joint.

"Nah, dude. No clue. There are no cameras in the garage. All they got was a shoe print in her blood. That there is some fucked up shit! Oh hey, do you mind if I smoke?" Rick asked.

Steve shuddered when Rick told him about the shoe print.

"Yeah, I'm okay. You can smoke away. Anything else on the news?" Steve calmly asked while nearing a full panic underneath.

"Not much. The po-po came out with a thing that talked about a serial killer who goes after online shit-posters. They found this dude in a canal, and another chick is missing. They're still clueless, as usual. Man, what kind of balls does it take to do something like that? I wish I had the balls this dude has. They probably all deserved it. Most of them do. Even Michelle. She was a real stuck-up, woke bitch. She also trolled like a bitch. Now, her account is locked. I checked." Rick smiled and winked, then took a long drag on his doobie.

Steve wondered if they all really did deserve it. Without the alcohol, Steve didn't know what to think. What had been such a clear driver to his revenge was now a muddled landscape of regret mixed with misery and guilt. And anguish. Unbearable anguish.

"I don't know, dude. I don't know. But hey, thanks for looking after me," Steve said.

"No problem, dude. You kept pissing and shitting yourself, so I got you diapers. I took some photos to blackmail you later. No big deal. I gotta clean this sofa now from all your horrid liquids. It smells as bad as you do," Rick said, laughing at Steve's worried and weary expression.

PART III

Another two weeks passed, and all mention of the Chatter Killer fell out of the news cycle. Steve fully expected a knock on the door for his arrest. It hadn't come, but he was convinced that he could be arrested at any time. He literally practiced pushing the thought out of his mind. It was the only way to stay sane since he couldn't drink anymore. The yearning for alcohol had mostly passed, but it was still always there.

His cell phone jiggled. It was June.

"Hey, honey, just checking in! See you next week?" June asked, sounding very upbeat. Steve liked the trend of June calling him honey. She had never really done that before.

"Of course!" he said. "I'm starting at my new job, and then I'll be back."

"I think you'll like the new gig, sweetheart! At least you've done it before," June said.

Steve had taken a job at another municipality as a low-level computer tech. Decent pay and the possibility of another retirement package. He had applied months ago, but fortunately, they called back shortly after he was sober. By then, he even had hair and thin eyebrows.

"Yeah, I think it will be a good change. Anything but unemployment and drinking is a good change," Steve said.

June and Steve said their goodbyes and hung up. He was glad that this nightmare was almost over, although the ever-present fear of arrest was right up there with the horror of killing Michelle. Before the murder, he giggled to himself at the thought of her other coworkers finding her rotting, bloated corpse under her car. Now, the same imagery wore him down layer by layer, and it was incessant.

PART IV

Steve roared, "TODAY IS THE DAY!" Rick rolled his eyes. "Things are going to start happening to me NOW!" He grinned as he quoted 'The Jerk.' Steve finally had a sense of humor again.

"You fuckturd, it wasn't that bad living here, was it?" Rick asked, seeming somewhat hopeful Steve would say no.

"Nah, man, you were great. I can't tell you how much all this meant to me. You really saw me through some rough patches," Steve said.

Rick nodded. "You bet I did! That piss was something else. My couch still smells like an old folk's mattress, you pissy fuck!"

Steve smiled, shook hands with Rick, and walked out to his car carrying his clothes, phone charger, and nothing else. As he pulled away, Steve continued to think about Michelle and her child.

He made the journey home and felt a wave of relief as he entered his quiet neighborhood. The differences between Steve's home and Rick's apartment were vast. The trash-filled streets had now given way to nicely mowed lawns and sculpted bushes. He was quick to note that his house looked quite nice. June and the kids had really kept the yard looking great. Pride beamed through him as he pulled up.

June was waiting on the front porch for Steve's return. She was not ashamed to admit that she was giddy inside, like a proverbial schoolgirl waiting for a date. Sex had been non-existent since he left, and she hoped that it had been the same for him.

Steve pulled up and saw June leap down the steps to the driveway in a flowery dress. It was one of the best things he had seen in months, given the past few months were an absolute horror show.

"Hey, there's my baby!" June yelled as she ran to greet the car. The kids soon joined them outside but stayed on the porch to let Mom and Dad do icky stuff.

"You know it!" Steve said. "I'm so glad to be home, you don't even know."

Steve went to grab his suitcase, but June pulled him away from the car and gave him a full lips and tongue treatment. Steve gasped a bit, then kissed her back harder. Perhaps June was a bit randy, he knew he was. Never once had he thought to sleep with somebody else—both on principle and on capability. Booze is a powerful sedative.

The two locked in an embrace until the kids called down to them.

"Break it up, please. This is embarrassing. Don't you have a bedroom or something?" Kathy said. Brian grunted in solidarity.

"Oh yeah, we do! Better put on a Barney tape!" Steve joked back as his kids came down to give him a hug. It wasn't much of a joke, really. That purple dinosaur had provided cover noise for years when the kids were younger.

Kathy rolled her eyes. "Welcome back, Dad. We're happy you're home," she said over her shoulder as she turned to leave. And with that, Kathy and Brian went back inside—Appearance made and attitude kept. Under the façade, they were really glad he was back, not just for them but for their mom.

They both watched their kids go back inside. "Emotional as usual," Steve said.

"Well, they have been. They're keeping up appearances for you. There have been many nights when I heard them both crying in their beds, and I had to console them. It was rough on them, too," June said.

Steve thought about this for a moment. His actions had far-reaching consequences. Some of which nobody else knew about. For now. The images of Michelle flashed across his consciousness, his intestines turned to ice, and his balls did their thing once again. Steve brought himself back to the present and hugged June, and then they walked inside. He hoped she wouldn't notice his anguish, which was almost overwhelming.

PART V

Steve was well into his first month at his new job, and it was going well. He had made a few new friends, and the pace of work was a bit low-key. But low-key was good at this point in his life. The last several months had been anything but—Mass murder being at the forefront.

Another workday finished, Steve parked the car and made his way up the path to his door, where he saw June waiting for him.

"I think we need to venture out for dinner," she said.

Steve walked inside and flopped into the new recliner that June had bought specifically for his return.

"Well, I think Marisol's is appropriate. It is about time we went back. The kids and I haven't eaten there since The Day," June continued.

Steve took a deep breath. This was asking a lot, and June knew it. "I really don't want to. I have PTMD. Post Traumatic Marisol's Disorder," Steve said.

She could see that he was partly serious. But she persisted. "I think it would do us good and put that event in the past where it belongs. I'm gathering up the kids. Let's go," June said as she walked up the stairs, not allowing Steve to reply. Any reply after that would be pointless. June was a determined wife. And with that, the decision was made, and off they went, with Steve dragging his feet the entire way.

"Anything you want, honey. Anything you want," Steve moped.

Since it was a weeknight, they got seated almost at once. Steve didn't recognize the hostess, but their favorite server saw them and directed them to her table.

"Hey! Long time no see, Rocky Balboa!" the server said. Steve couldn't remember her name at all but tried to hide it. They didn't wear name tags, as many had been working there for a generation. But this did not help Steve.

"Hey there, yourself!" Steve said while trying to smile. He was indeed having PTMD. "How's it been going?"

The server rolled her eyes with near-Kathy precision. "Oh, Papi. Ever since that big fight and being on the news, we actually got very busy. You were good for business!"

"Well, my pleasure. It just mostly ruined my life for the last four months. But other than that, it was okay," Steve joked while images of his victims flew through his mind, quietly tormenting him.

They ordered their usuals, and the kids asked for Mexican Cokes. That was a first. When it came to what Steve wanted to drink, he asked for water.

"Wait, no margaritas for you? Are you for real?" the server asked, making a fake, shocked face and grabbing her collar.

"No, I'm good," Steve said. "Maybe next time. I'm trying to lose weight."

As he told the casual lie, June patted his leg. He didn't really need reassurance but smiled and patted her leg back.

The server laughed and left to place the order. After two baskets of chips and a large bowl of guac, a huge serving tray of molten hot food was brought to the table. It was as good and satisfying as he remembered. June noticed Steve smile at his meal and again patted his leg.

"See? This was a good idea, wasn't it?" she said.

Steve nodded, then dug into the chimichanga topped with beef gravy.

"You're right, it was a good idea. For a woman," Steve smirked.

This prompted a double eye roll from June and Kathy and a brief grunt of affirmation from Brian. Almost from the start of the dinner, their eyes hadn't moved much from their screens.

"So, you still surfing social media?" Steve asked them both.

"Nah," Kathy said. "I just go around looking at what other girls are posting on what they wear. It's like a lot more positive. I'm done with Chatter." After her brief interaction with the real world over, Kathy looked down again and resumed scrolling. While that seemed like social media to Steve, he hoped at least it wasn't toxic.

"So, what about you?" Steve asked Brian. He looked up after a few seconds.

"What?" Brian said. Steve's words had not yet been computed.

"So, what are you doing? Sesame Street reruns?" Steve laughed. Brian engaged a bit more at this point.

"Nah, I'm into game streaming. Some of these guys actually make money from people watching them play games! It's awesome!" Brian said, a sudden sparkle igniting in his eyes. The sparkle was met by a worried scowl from June.

"We've discussed this, Brian. You're not allowed to stream under any circumstance until you're 18. It is just not happening," June retorted. It was obvious that this topic was a bit of a sore point. Steve saw Brian's eyes dull.

"Hey! Maybe it's something we can talk about, right?" Steve said. June turned her scowl to Steve and squeezed his leg. He silently replied by assuring her that it would just be a discussion for now, all from his body language. Parents had to communicate pseudo-telepathically at these moments.

Brian smiled and nodded and went back to watching DeathScream69 walk into a troll's cave. It was quite a battle.

The check came and was paid, and Steve left a sizeable tip as usual. He didn't like to think about it as a bribe, but it kinda was. The service remained excellent, and the tip helped. It also helped the staff, which Steve and June always kept in mind.

There were three large televisions behind the bar that Steve would occasionally watch between bites. June could not tolerate facing them, as she found them pointless and distracting. One of them had on the local news while the others were playing sports. A 'Breaking News' graphic, in all its glory and excitement, suddenly caught Steve's attention. The banner read, "Chatter Killer Caught."

Steve's mouth dropped open as he digested what he had just read. Although he couldn't hear the TV, the closed captioning was on.

"Phoenix police have finally caught who they believe is the Chatter Killer, the alleged killer responsible for the deaths of Michelle Connor, a City of Phoenix employee, and Frankie Martinez, a local activist and artist. The last known victim, Felix Champion, another local activist, was found last Friday. Police have also tied the disappearance of Amber Hardy, a neighborhood barista who disappeared two months ago, to the suspect. City of Phoenix Police Detective Luis Garcia broke the case," the newscaster said.

The detective appeared on the screen, gently smoothing his hair as he responded to an off-camera question. Steve had no memory of Felix, and his murder only happened last week. After his painful detox, he was fully aware of where he was and what he had done, so this crime was a mystery.

"With a partial bloody shoe print at Michelle Connor's death scene and cell phone records placing the suspect at the scene of the Champion murder, the final piece of the puzzle was a clear set of fingerprints and DNA evidence found at the Champion scene. The suspect was apprehended with shoes that matched the prints left at the Connor's scene. The evidence implicates Richard 'Rick' Adams as our primary suspect. Mr. Adams was a coworker of Ms. Connor, and many City of Phoenix employees have come forward with testimony on the tense relationship the two shared. Adams also had prior arrests for drug possession, and his prints were a perfect match to the ones found. The people can rest assured that justice will be served."

Steve watched in amazement as the footage showed Rick being taken from his apartment. Rick was yelling something in normal Rick crazy-man fashion, but the subtitles didn't spell it out. Nor would the producers want it to. He could tell that there were a lot of "fuck yous" and insults thrown at the cops who were roughing him into the car. Police had laid out the evidence of a knife, some duct tape, and a yellow pair of Crocs. *Steve's Crocs.*

By this time, June had noticed a change in Steve's demeanor. She turned in time to see the video of Rick's arrest.

"Oh my! Isn't that your coworker? The guy you stayed with?" June asked, now suddenly alarmed.

Steve sat silent for a moment. "Yeah. He apparently killed some people, including Michelle. Holy shit." The lie tore at Steve's soul, yet it felt like a dark blanket had been pulled from his regret. Steve knew he could never forgive himself for what he had done, but he didn't see this one coming. He didn't want Rick to take the fall for what he had done, but he did kill someone else. He was Steve's copycat. And Steve was ashamed of his relief.

The story continued with the newscaster finishing the piece.

"The motive in this case remains unclear, but early statements from the suspect seem to indicate that revenge for online postings was the primary motivation. Each victim had posted on a variety of topics over the history of their accounts, with many focusing on social issues. So far, the police are unable to find a clear path that would drive Rick Adams, 35, to murder. Mr Adams has denied the killings, but the evidence all points back to him, say police. This is Karen Black, channel 10. Back to you…"

PART VI

Steve pulled the car into the driveway and sat while the children went inside. June looked over at Steve with a furrowed brow.

"Is everything okay? I know this is a shock," June said.

Steve nodded. "Yeah. I'll be okay. I'd rather not talk about it for a while if that's alright."

June patted Steve on the leg and opened the car door. "Come on. Let's go inside for a little mommy-papi time." June smiled mischievously and then got out of the car.

Steve stayed for a good five minutes, absorbing the turn of events. He wouldn't have believed that Rick was capable of a seemingly random but yet targeted murder. He had apparently killed Felix after all. Using Steve's shoes and being Rick's stupid self, he failed to cover his tracks. Not that Steve was proud of the tracks that he covered himself. Finally, putting his thoughts to rest, he opened the door and made his way to the bedroom.

Getting ready for sleep and adjusting his CPAP, Steve sat at the edge of the bed for more than a few minutes. June noted this and realized that fun time was no longer in the picture. Tonight had been a lot. Thinking about how to break the moment, she remembered her purchase.

"Hey. I couldn't find your Crocs after you came back, so I got you some new ones."

June went into the closet to get the shoes and laid them at Steve's feet. They were a pair of bright yellow Crocs.

Steve looked down, and the viper pit in his stomach returned for a moment. On one hand, they were a thoughtful gift from June, and at least they weren't covered in blood. On the other hand, they would be a constant reminder of the past few months. Rick had used his shoes to commit the next murder, which Steve had accidentally left behind.

"Thank you, honey. I really appreciate the thoughtfulness," Steve murmured. June nodded.

"You're welcome, sweetheart. Yard work this weekend? You can break in your new shoes!" she said in a soft voice.

He nodded silently as his head hit the pillow. "Anything you want, honey. Anything you want."

EPILOGUE

"A body has been found in central Phoenix with what appears to be at least ten stab wounds. Phoenix PD discovered a note at the crime scene referencing social media posts by the victim. While this is not the work of the Chatter Killer, who is now awaiting sentencing, the details are similar. More information to follow."

Phoenix Police PIO (@PhxPolice)

Detective Luis Garcia walked around the victim, observing the details. The stab wounds were obvious, and there were many. The note was taped to the body. It was a screenshot of the victim's post.

"I guess this is the post that sent the perp over the edge," an officer said.

Luis pondered. "Oh, who the fuck knows which one it was. Whoever did this was obviously unhinged, don't you think?"

"No shit," the officer laughed, then walked away. Luis bent down with his flashlight to look at the note. It was about someone who had apparently shown up to a rally. He couldn't make the rest out, but evidence hadn't been collected yet, and soon, they would know more about the motive. Maybe. Hopefully.

Luis stood up as another officer came to look at the body.

"Do you think it's related to you know who?" he asked.

"Maybe. If it is, I think we have a problem on our hands," Luis said, shaking his head.

"Well, you da man, Detective! You solved the last one. You da man!" the officer chortled.

Luis was not so sure about that, especially after the last investigation and how long it took to develop real evidence. Maybe this one would be different. Maybe not.

As he reached his car and sat down, his mind wandered to Rick, the Chatter Killer. He wondered what could drive a person to do what he did. And what drove this one? Maybe society was in the process of unraveling?

"Well, I've got more things to handle than worry about the world's problems," Luis said to himself as he slowly headed back home through the dark Phoenix streets.

- 183 -

- To Be Continued -